PERSPECTIVE

A DARK TALE of HOPE ✳

PERSPECTIVE
A DARK TALE of HOPE

Amanda Hovseth

Synecdoche Publishing

For information contact:
Synecdoche Publishing
synecdochepublishing.wordpress.com

Cover and Book Design by Amanda Hovseth

Soft Cover ISBN: 978-1-945018-10-7
E-book ISBN: 978-1-945018-11-4

Library of Congress Control Number: 2017912210

3rd Edition: 2017

DEDICATED TO

Daniel Timothy Hovseth
(My Daddy)

For being the best, eccentric, apologetics-studying, truth-speaking, dad a girl couldn't even dream of asking for.

Like a shooting star, he burned fast and bright, leaving his mark across the Heavens.

✻ *Prologue*

DECLAN'S MIND RACED. *What's happening? Who are these people? Where are they taking me?* He struggled to catch his breath through the rough fabric which was covering his head as someone's hand on his shoulder forcefully guided him down unevenly laid out stairs.

Slivers of warm and flickering light reached his eyes through a few loose strands of fabric. *Fire*, he decided. *Torches?* The air around him grew cooler and cooler, and he thought, with dry humor, of how inconsiderate his kidnappers were in not grabbing his jacket on the way out.

Finally, after what seemed like ages of stumbling down uneven stairs, the ground leveled. The man guiding him shoved him forward one last time and said gruffly, "Wait there, stand still and don't move." Declan sighed and chewed on his lower lip as he tried to listen closely to his surroundings while mulling over what had just happened.

All he could remember was the sound of hushed voices waking him in the middle of the night. He had sat up quickly to turn on his bedside light, but the second he had moved, six men-shaped shadows pinned him down. One of the men had shoved the dirty bag over his head as two others had bound his hands with rope before picking him up, rushing out of his house, and throwing him into some sort of vehicle. He had tried to ask them questions, but every time he spoke someone smacked him on the back of the head and told him to quiet down. So, he had eventually decided silence was his best option, and now he simply waited.

"Oww! Hey sunshine, chill already, I'm moving, okay? How 'bout you blindfold yourself, see how speedy *you* are, huh?"

The voice had come from Declan's left. *I'm not the only one?* He wasn't sure if this caused relief or made him even more perplexed.

"You know, if this is a ransom situation you're out of luck, buddy," the boy to his left said loudly. "My dad is a stingy old crony. You won't get nothin' outa him."

Declan couldn't resist smiling; he had just been thinking the exact same thing about his father.

"If you really want money, you should've kidnapped my dad's financial advisor… or his secretary," the boy added with a chuckle.

Suddenly, the bag on Declan's head was yanked off. He blinked as he took in his surroundings. They were in a large room which appeared to be carved out of stone. It had wide, arched doorways and evenly spaced torches for light. Somewhere in the distance he heard a steady dripping, but he pushed that to the back of his mind, because surrounding him were at least thirty men shrouded in black cloaks with black hoods pulled down to the bridges of their noses.

"Hah!" the boy next to him exclaimed. "Joke's on you. Last I heard, you need a virgin for this type of creepy sacrifice thing."

Declan turned to look at his companion. The tall, blond, blue-eyed boy had a cocky smile pasted to his face. He caught Declan's eye, winked, then leaned over and whispered in his ear, "Can't let 'em see you sweat." Declan simply raised his eyebrows in response. "Nice; a pro I see," the boy said with a grin and a nod.

"Listen up," a man's voice boomed throughout the room like rolling thunder as the hooded men parted to allow him to step forward.

The man moved slowly, assisted by a tall, crooked cane. When, at last, he reached the front of the group he stood directly opposite the two boys, lifted his head, and removed his hood. The elderly man had wrinkles all over his face and eyes as cold as ice. But Declan noticed something more—something familiar.

He had certainly seen this man before—maybe in a photo—but he didn't have time to contemplate it because the man began to speak.

"Congratulations," the man's voice dragged as slow as his walk. "You young men have officially come of the proper age to join our brotherhood."

The man paused for an awkward amount of time. Declan found himself wondering if he should say something, decided against it, and then was surprised to realize that the boy next to him stayed quiet as well.

"The two of you will be entering high school in a few weeks and it is time for you to start thinking of your futures. You have been blessed with the blood that flows through your veins. It is the same blood that flowed through your fathers before you and your fathers' fathers.

It is the blood of great men who have reigned throughout history in their circle of influence. Leaders wrought with success and dignity that were strengthened and supported by the band of brothers represented here. Today is your day to join our ranks—a family knit together by the bonds of blood and united in our desire for greatness." The man paused while another man handed him an ornate goblet encrusted in gems. "This challis is filled with the blood of your forefathers, drink of it, and the initiation process will begin. Drink of it, and you will never stand alone in the world. Drink of it, and you will be destined to succeed. Your future is in your hands. What do you choose?"

Declan's throat became dry as he stared at the goblet outstretched toward him, but his thoughts were interrupted as the blond boy next to him cleared his throat.

"Just so you know, Dad," he said to the crowd, "I wasn't serious about that crony thing."

Declan smiled as one of the hooded men sighed deeply. *Blood of my forefathers… what could it hurt?*

❋ *Chapter 1*

Saturday, October 15, 2011

SHE UNDERSTOOD WHAT they were asking her and she understood why; she just wished they would stop.

"Destiny, please try to remember." Her mom was sitting next to her hospital bed. Everyone else had left the room in hopes that she would feel more comfortable if it were just her and her mom. They were right, she did feel more comfortable. "There is no way I can understand what you're feeling right now, but there is one thing I do know. The doctors say Rohypnol often causes memory loss, so you may not remember anything that happened after it got into your system. But, you have to try to at least remember enough for us to figure out who did this to you, okay?"

Destiny nodded.

Mrs. Ackerman smiled. "Most important of all though,

you need to remember that your dad and I still love you very much and we want you to know that you are not to blame for this situation." She started tearing up and stumbling over her words. "You are everything we could ask for in a daughter... and I... I just can't believe someone would do this to you!" She covered her mouth to try and stifle and involuntary sob.

Destiny reached out and took her other hand. "It's okay mom... I know." Destiny struggled to get more out, but didn't have to because her mom realized she needed to pull herself together since she was supposed to be the one that was "being strong".

"Now," Mrs. Ackerman cleared her throat, sat up straighter, and dried her eyes with a tissue. "Let's review what we do know. You've already told us that the last thing you remember is walking to your car from the library. That's when you started to go weak and blacked out. The doctors found traces of the Rohypnol in your water bottle, and you said you had just refilled it at the library drinking fountain, so someone must have slipped it in while you were there. Did you ever leave your stuff alone?"

"Yes, I had to pee."

"So, you had to *go to the restroom*," she emphasized, never missing a chance to teach formality to her daughter, "and left your stuff alone. Unfortunately, the library does not have security cameras and the librarians didn't pay enough attention to even realize you were there, so they have been no help. Did you happen to notice anyone suspicious?"

"No, I didn't see anyone fishy there." She said truthfully. "They must have been very sneaky."

"Okay." Mrs. Ackerman paused, pursed her lips and

stared at the ceiling. "Did you notice anyone in the parking lot as you left for home?"

"No." Destiny looked down at the sheets and started rubbing a soft, cottony one between her fingers. "I… I'm just… tired."

Mrs. Ackerman refocused her eyes on her daughter and reached up to brush Destiny's hair from her face, but Destiny subconsciously maneuvered her head out of reach. "Oh," her mom stammered and gently took Destiny's hand instead. "I'm sorry… I didn't mean to make you uncomfortable." Tears returned to her eyes.

"It's okay, Mom. You didn't do anything wrong. I think though, I think… is it okay if I just take a nap now?" Destiny tried to force herself to give reassuring eye contact, but instead she ended up looking at the ridiculous painting of brightly colored, random shapes on the wall behind her mom and then returned to the cotton sheet on her bed.

"Yes, honey, that sounds like a good idea." She smiled and patted Destiny's hand. "I'll go find your dad and see if he wants to get some lunch in the cafeteria while we let you rest. If you need us just let the nurse know and we will return right away."

Destiny smiled at her. "Okay, Mom. Thanks."

Her mom stood up and headed through the door, but before she closed it, she turned back to say, "I love you, Hun!"

"Love you too, Mom," Destiny responded as she rolled over onto her side and pulled the blankets up under her chin.

As the door closed, Destiny shut her eyes and was bombarded with the previous night's events. Tears began to pour out between her eyelids. *Where did I go wrong? What*

7

did I do to deserve this? She raised her left hand in front of her face. Her purity ring shone brightly, still on her finger. "No sex before marriage" is what most people took it to mean, but she took it even further. Until last night she hadn't even been kissed. *It's all ruined.*

Anger burned within her and the tears came faster. She twisted the ring off her finger and placed it on the bedside table but continued to stare at it. Deep inside a voice told her it would still be okay to wear the ring. *This was forced on me, not my choice, no one would hold it against me.* But an even louder voice said, *It doesn't matter if I chose it or not; I am dirty now, used, destroyed.* She pulled the pillow from beneath her head, covered her mouth with it, and screamed at the top of her lungs, took another breath and just kept screaming until she had nothing left inside. Then she threw the pillow at the wall across the room.

An ironic chuckle escaped her mouth as she realized she only hurt herself with that action because now she had no pillow. "Great, now I'm going crazy too," she mumbled under her breath as she bundled up one of her many blankets into pillow form and lay back down.

"At least I'm not diseased," she tried to encourage herself, venom tingeing her voice. "The doctors say that's great news, very rare not to be worse off in this type of situation, high probability I could even be dead now, or at least terribly injured."

THEN WHY DO I FEEL LIKE NOTHING BUT GARBAGE COVERED IN A SKIN SHELL? She screamed silently. She closed her eyes, clenched her fists, and imagined the garbage inside being consumed in a blazing fire.

"They have to pay for what they took from me," she spoke aloud again, then thought, *How dare they? They should have known better! It's not what I wanted; it wasn't their decision to make. It was mine and they ignored me!* He *ignored me!*

I have to turn them in! She crossed her arms decidedly, took a deep breath, and again closed her eyes—actually feeling like sleeping, but tears continued to slowly drain from them, because she knew better.

She wouldn't be turning them in. She couldn't turn them in. The very same guys who had done this to her had now become her greatest hope for things to not get worse. She would tell no one.

All she could do was cry herself to sleep.

Chapter 2

THE HOSPITAL LOOKED like a castle, lighting up the night through its many windows—warm and welcoming to weary or downtrodden travelers, housing the sick and dying, trying to bring hope, life, and second chances to the world. But Declan could not enter it. More than anything he wanted to go running through those sliding glass doors, up the stairs, and into room 320 where she rested. He wanted to let her know she was all he had ever cared about, all he wanted in this life and he would never let anyone hurt her, he would do anything to keep her safe. And he had done that. Hadn't he?

An icy breeze slithered its way through his suit jacket, causing him to shiver. He had been standing in this hospital parking lot since he first heard she had woken up, just staring at the third floor, wondering which window belonged to her, debating whether or not it would be a good idea to visit her.

Maybe she would be happy to see him; relieved, since he had made the hard decisions for her and now she could relax. Of course she would be grateful. She had been trapped by her archaic beliefs and she wouldn't have been able to choose the route toward safety on her own. It was the only logical choice, really. She had to at least understand that.

But something inside told him it may not be that simple.

She didn't see the world the same way he saw it. She saw life as having meaning and purpose; she had values and morals; she cared strongly and loved deeply; and she may have preferred death over betraying her convictions.

Declan's dark eyes stared at the cap-toes of his black Prada bluchers, now covered in dust from standing outside for so long. He ruffled his shaggy ebony hair with his right hand as he thought, *why couldn't she have just agreed with me, gone along with the plan, then we could both be happy; celebrating our clever use of a loophole together. We wouldn't have to be in this situation.*

Just then a glistening limo pulled up as one of the back passenger-side windows was rolling down.

"Declan." Alexander, one of his crew members, poked his short-haired blond head through the open window, his blue eyes shining. "We figured we'd find you here. Come on, man. You made the right decision, stop creeper-ing the hospital. Let's go to your place and watch one of those over-the-top comedies Jesse loves to force on us."

"I don't know," Declan responded. "She is not like us; she's different. She probably hates me now…" His voice broke at the vocal acknowledgment of his worst fear and he went back to staring at his shoes.

Lex gave an exasperated groan. "Well, Romeo, you

aren't going to solve any problems freezing to death out here. Come on; get in the car. I'll make—buy some popcorn."

Declan sighed. He had to agree with Lex; he'd been standing here too long. It was time to go. At least he knew she would be safe in the hospital.

As he climbed into the vehicle with Lex and the other two members of his crew, they all slapped him on the back, saying things like: "Yeah, bro, it'll be all right"; "No worries man, we already sent her some classy flowers and a cute teddy bear from you"; and, "We'll all get wasted tonight, help take your mind off things". Declan nodded half-heartedly to each of them as he took his seat, and eventually the car grew silent as the driver headed toward his home in the Paradise Estates.

Declan allowed himself to relax in the warmth and familiarity of the vehicle while staring out the window at the passing buildings with their neon lights and crowded advertisements. It all seemed so empty and meaningless. A gigantic weight pressed in on his chest as he realized he may have lost her for good. He may have done something she viewed as unforgiveable. She had been the only piece of hope he had found in the world; a pinprick of light in the tedium of his day-to-day. He could be left with nothing. He pressed his head against the chilled window and allowed the emotional and physical exhaustion of the last twenty-four hours to pull his eyes closed as he contemplated how the past had gotten him here, beginning with the day this all started. The day he had first met her.

August 1999

"Declan, stop fidgeting with your tie, it makes you seem vulnerable," the governor commanded his son from across the vehicle.

"But, father, no one else will be dressed like this, I will be weird." Declan moaned with a pout.

His father, Mr. Rayner, was a tall, intimidating man with a strong chin and defined jawline. He sighed as he leaned forward to straighten the tie Declan had just jumbled up. "We already discussed this. You are entering the first grade, and the habits you form now will influence the rest of your life, so you have to get used to dressing like the person you want to become; which, of course, is a winner."

"Why can't I go to my old school? I don't know anyone here."

"Well, Declan, you are probably too young to understand this now, but I need to appear to relate to the people I serve, so I need to experience their lives on some level. My advisers tell me the best way to do that is to have my child in the same education system as the majority of the voters' children. That way they can trust me to make good decisions for the public education system. This means private school is no longer an option, and I do not want to hear you complain about it anymore. You will make new friends here and will still get to see your old friends quite often at social events."

The car pulled up in front of his new school and Declan glared disdainfully at the red brick building as his father ushered him out of the vehicle and through the front entrance.

"Come now, son. I don't have much time; let's get you to your classroom."

The walk to his room and meeting his teacher was a blur. Before he knew it, his father had left him sitting alone at a tiny, creaky desk with ten minutes to spare before the bell rang. Declan sighed and folded his hands on top of his desk to wait patiently, but instead of calming down, he noticed a couple of boys who were sitting to his right, staring at him and laughing.

"Get lost on your way to snobs-ville?" the blond one with a crew cut and dirty sneakers taunted, eliciting loud boisterous laughter from the rest of the class.

Declan felt his face begin to flush so he lowered his head to stare at his hands as he tried to fight back tears and contemplated the quickest route out of the room. But his plans were interrupted by the confident voice of a young girl.

"What's so funny 'bout that?" she demanded. "Sounds like you're the ones bein' a snob." The rest of the room quickly fell silent. "Besides," she added, "I like his tie, it's bright green, a very cool color."

Declan could have sworn he actually heard the other kids start to agree with her. So, he relaxed a little, slowly lifted his eyes, and turned toward her voice.

She also sat to his right, but farther toward the back of the room. She wore her dark brown hair pulled into two French braids, and her brown eyes had a hint of green in them. She sported sparkly pink sneakers, a fluffy layered bright green skirt, a T-shirt with a picture of Superman on it, and a bright smile aimed directly at him.

Declan's father's words popped into his mind. "Dress like the person you want to become." He glanced at the name tag on her desk. *Destiny… Destiny, my Superman.*

☀ *Chapter 3*

Saturday, October 15, 2011

DECLAN SIGHED AS he remembered how relieved he had been to no longer feel alone at that new school. Then he allowed his mind to wander forward a few years from their first meeting to another great memory.

Saturday, September 21, 2002

Declan sat on the patio watching his classmates who were screaming out laughter at unbelievably high octaves as they ran throughout the yard. He was in third grade now and should be enjoying himself with them. After all, it was his birthday party—well, one of his birthday parties. His father had seen fit to have two parties: one for the elite; classy and always held at some resort for an entire weekend; and one for the families of his classmates, held in his backyard for a few hours. This party was the latter and complete with a giant, inflatable bouncy castle.

"You have to cater to the different types of people according to their specific tastes," Mr. Rayner always told him as he explained the value of separate parties. "The parents of your classmates will not want to pay for a weekend stay at a resort and our other friends will think a backyard party is too simple. This way everyone is happy!"

Yeah, everyone except me, Declan thought, then immediately felt guilty for thinking it. *This isn't as bad as it could be though* he reasoned—to balance the scale.

In fact, things had been going pretty well. When he had first started classes at the public school, some of the other kids had picked on him; but that didn't last long, partly because they enjoyed being invited to stuff like this. However, Declan knew that wasn't the biggest reason, because they were all aware that even if they were mean to him they would be invited anyway. The governor had to make a good impression and could not leave anyone out. The biggest reason they did not tease him, of course, was Destiny.

Declan smiled when she came to mind. She had become his best friend at school—actually, kind of his only real friend. She, on the other hand, was friends with everybody to some extent. She had a knack for finding ways to relate to anyone and she was always easygoing and happy. Unless, of course, others decided to be mean. Then she stood up to them until they stopped. Declan couldn't think of even one time when someone didn't listen when she spoke. Something about her just made people want to follow her lead.

Declan thought it was her smile, people just wanted her to be happy so they could see her smile. But, no matter the reason for her effectiveness, every time the other kids attempted to mock him, Destiny was there to put a swift end to it. She really did not like to see people get hurt and Declan could not be more grateful.

"Sorry I'm late."

Declan jumped in surprise. Destiny had taken a seat right next to him and he hadn't even noticed during his stare-off with the bouncy castle.

"Here, I brought you a present," she stated proudly as she handed him a small rectangular box wrapped in a paper bag which was covered in colorful hand-drawn balloons, party hats, and confetti. Then, right in the middle of the decorations was "DECLAN" written in large bubble letters.

Declan chuckled as he examined the wrapping job. "Did you wrap this yourself?"

"Yes," she responded with a scowl, "wrapping paper is expensive. This is all I had cuz paper bags are free when we go shopping."

"No," he started, "I mean… I like it, your drawings are pretty."

She pressed her lips together and smiled. "Okay then, thanks, I guess… how 'bout you open it now?" she said with a quick clap of her hands and fast skootch closer to him.

"Oh, yeah, I guess I could." Declan flipped the gift over to its bottom and carefully peeled off the tape, trying his best to not tear the paper, and slid the box out. He glanced up at Destiny. Her eyes were open so wide in anticipation it made him smile, a smile that only grew as he lifted the lid to reveal the gift. A silky tie gleamed up at him, but not a normal boring tie like the ones his mother always bought him. It had a bright and colorful background with a picture of Batman striking a pose right in the middle.

"I figured since you're always complaining 'bout having to wear ties, maybe this one would make it better for you," Destiny explained. "Of course, I almost got you Superman since he's the best superhero ever. But, I figured since it's your birthday I'd do what you'd want and get you a lamer one." She rolled her eyes in mock annoyance.

Declan laughed. "Yeah, right. You say that, but really you picked Batman since secretly you know he is the best. You just do not want to admit it."

This was an ongoing argument between them. Declan hadn't cared much for superheroes until he met Destiny but he figured he might as well give them a chance if it meant he'd have something more to talk to her about. But, when he learned about Batman, he did genuinely gain an interest in the characters.

Destiny claimed the only reason he liked Batman was because Batman was a rich guy and so was Declan. She insisted that if Declan weren't rich, Superman would have been his hero of choice as well. She believed that Superman was as close to perfect as they come; and if you were going to have someone rescue you, you would want the one with the better odds. Declan disagreed. He liked Batman because he was just a normal guy doing what he thought needed to be done, even if he didn't have any special powers—although he would be lying if he said the money thing wasn't an issue, because it was. The idea that Batman was wealthy and chose to fight for the good of all men instead of just trying to trick people into thinking he cared (like his father did), made him feel as if there was some hope for his future. It allowed him to think that maybe he could be wealthy and actually care for people— perhaps even help them.

Destiny sighed. "Whatever you say, birthday boy. For today anyway," she added as she elbowed him playfully. "So, do you like it?"

"Yes, I do! Thank you!" he responded, and it was the truth. Under normal circumstances his parents would not have let him buy or wear a tie that looked so unprofessional, but if it was a gift from one of his father's "citizens", then they would have to let him wear it—at least to school. Not wearing it would be rude. "It is the perfect gift," he added as he tucked it back into the box alongside the wrapping paper which he had folded neatly, intending to save it as well.

With a nod, Destiny responded, "Cool." Then she changed the subject. "Why aren't you playing in the jumpy castle with everyone else?"

Declan's mood instantly dropped. "I was, and it was fun, but then someone got the bright idea to spray water inside to make it slippery, and now I cannot jump in it."

"Why not? It's just water; you'll dry off."

"Yeah, I will, but not my jacket." He held his arms out as if to accentuate his point. "It is suede, and if it gets wet it will be ruined."

"Then take it off," Destiny reasoned.

"I can't." Declan crossed his arms sternly. "Father insisted I leave it on for the whole party because it will set me apart as dignified and mature so all the other parents will admire how well-mannered I am and make him look good or something."

Destiny looked thoughtful. "This just means we have to find a way for you to be able to take the jacket off and still seem mature." She clasped her hand on his knee, excitedly. "I have an idea!"

"What?" Declan questioned, sitting up straight and

furrowing his brow as he watched her stand and motion for him to follow.

"It's something I've seen my dad do for my mom," she explained as she led him into the house where most of the parents were mingling. "Your dad's gotta see it though; how 'bout you introduce me to him?"

Declan hesitated, but she grabbed his hand and pulled him forward and he didn't want to disappoint her. He scanned the room for his father and found him standing by the fireplace among a large group of people, looking as if he were having a positively wonderful afternoon.

The children maneuvered their way across the room until Declan stood next to his father with Destiny by his side.

"Now, here is the man of the hour!" Mr. Rayner boasted at their arrival, patting Declan on the back and receiving the attention of all the surrounding adults.

"How do your pals like the party?"

"It is great Father; they really enjoy the castle," Declan responded. "I wanted you to meet my friend Destiny," he said while motioning toward her with his right hand. "She just arrived here a few minutes ago."

Destiny stepped toward the governor and held out her hand. "It is great to finally meet you, sir," she claimed politely, with a bright smile on her face.

The man let out a pleased chuckle as he brought his left hand to his chest and extended his right one to shake her hand. "Well, the honor is mine. It pleases me to see Declan making such well-mannered friends. I trust you are enjoying yourself here?"

"Oh, yes sir, I am!" she stated earnestly, then paused as if to think, and crossed her arms together in front of her. "I just wish I had remembered my jacket. I always forget it and end up chilly no matter where I go." She shot a quick glance at Declan and he immediately understood what she was doing.

Mr. Rayner scowled in concern. "Perhaps I should turn the heat up a little…"

Destiny quickly responded, "Oh no sir, that's not needed. It's not this place, it's just me. Mom says it's because I'm a girl. She says it's part of the job description; girls are always colder, and that's why I should remember my jacket. It's my own fault for forgetting it."

Mr. Rayner smiled, humored by her reasoning, and Declan saw his opportunity.

"Well, that is no reason for you to be cold for the entire party." Declan scowled. "Here, you should take my jacket," he stated while unbuttoning his jacket. Then he held it out to help her slip it on.

This elicited a loud ruckus of "aww's" and "how adorable's" from the crowd. Declan even heard someone say, "Now that's a well-raised boy; taught to respect a woman." After the jacket sat safely on Destiny, Declan risked a glance at his father and noted, to his relief, that his father glowed with pride, his head held high from all the positive responses. Declan grinned, amazed Destiny's plan had worked.

"Thank you, Declan." Destiny beamed at him. "Now I'm all cozy."

"No problem at all." He smiled back.

Declan felt a hand on his shoulder. "That's my boy, being a man! You two kids run along now and have some fun with the rest of your classmates."

"Yes, sir," Destiny agreed as she turned to leave.

"Thank you, Father," Declan stated as he hurried after Destiny.

Once they stepped outside Declan jumped up and down. "That was amazing! You are a genius!"

"Yep," Destiny chirped while grinning smugly, "and now I'm also all warm and cozy, and that means it's time for you to do some slip-n-slide jumping!"

"Are you sure? But, now *you* cannot come…" Declan realized with concern.

"Yeah, I don't like getting wet. Plus, it's your birthday; you need to at least give it a try."

"Okay, but I will not be long. Don't leave without telling me."

Destiny laughed. "I can't leave; I have to keep your jacket warm," she called after him as he ran toward the group of kids going crazy in the castle.

Later that night, as Declan lay in bed trying to fall asleep, it dawned on him that this was the most fun he had ever had on one of his birthdays. Destiny had gone out of her way to make sure he enjoyed himself. No one else had even thought twice about how he might be doing. He would definitely never forget how she looked sitting on the patio wearing his jacket and laughing at his antics in the bouncy castle, and, some day, he would do his best to return the favor.

Chapter 4

Friday, October 14, 2011

DESTINY GROANED LOUDLY as she packed her belongings into her backpack and then took a long drink from her water bottle. It had been a tough day, and she had come to the library in hopes that the quiet atmosphere would allow her to clear her mind and get some homework done. Unfortunately, it had the opposite effect, creating freedom for her mind to overload and run wild. Senior year was proving to be tough enough without adding this day to the mix. No matter what she did, she just couldn't shake the conversation she had earlier that day with Declan.

~

"…I know it sounds crazy and you think it is extreme. Believe me; I would not have brought it up unless I thought it was our best option." Declan's voice rang even and clear as he tried to reason with her. "Tomorrow afternoon the guys and I are expected to be on our way to New York for a business convention with our fathers. We will be gone for two weeks. I cannot look after you from New York, and by the time I get back it may be too late. You need protection, and unless you agree to this proposal, I cannot protect you. This is just a little thing that has to happen before I can use all the resources we have to offer."

Destiny's head buzzed and her pulse raced as she stared at him with widened eyes. "What kind of crazy organization is this?" She looked down at her ring and nervously twirled it on her finger. Her voice wavered as she asked softly, "Who do they think they are… that they could ask this of someone?"

"It is not like they ever really planned on asking it; but it does provide us with the perfect loophole. It would be foolish to not take advantage of it."

Destiny's hands froze in mid-ring twirl as she looked up at Declan and furrowed her brow. "Foolish? Really?"

Declan felt his heart sinking into his gut as he made eye-contact with her. He had expected some push-back to his plan and was prepared with various potential rebuttals, but Destiny's reaction wasn't leaving him with much wiggle room. *If only she had been at the* meeting, he thought, *then she might understand how lucky we are to have this option.* His mind wandered back to the discussion from the night before, when he had petitioned for the board members of his club to cancel their business trip.

~   ~   ~

"We have taken your request into consideration," a man at the head of the room wearing a long, flowing robe and tall, dark hat said in a deep, booming voice, "and the bottom line is this business trip could set you and the other members of your group onto a very successful career track. Even more, this girl you are telling us about has no significant importance to the goals of our group. She is not related to you nor married to you. Therefore, we have concluded that her safety is not your responsibility or even your first priority. We cannot grant permission for you to exclude yourself from this trip, and, even more so, to pull your fellow members out of it."

Declan looked around the room at the pursed-lipped, wrinkly-faced men who were nodding in agreement. He fervently tapped his right foot, bit his bottom lip, and rubbed his palms against his thighs before setting them flat on the table in front of him and standing up. "You say she has no significant importance?" He narrowed his eyes. "Well, what if she joined us? What if she was initiated?"

The man with the tall hat coughed as the room grew silent. "Initiated?" He laughed and motioned around the room. "Do you see any females here? What makes you think that is an option?"

Declan hesitated as he looked from the older man to his father. Out of curiosity Mr. Rayner raised an eyebrow and nodded for him to continue. "In the original code of the brotherhood there is a clause that states females may be initiated by submitting themselves entirely to the currently active chapter."

"Really? And how might a female do that?" a squeaky voiced gentleman to his left asked.

Declan cleared his throat and looked down at the table as he answered, "It says females submit themselves sexually."

The room sat in silence for a couple of seconds before everyone burst out into laughter, but Declan's determination grew, and he pushed forward.

"This girl I am talking about believes in saving herself for marriage." The room slowly grew quiet again as they started listening. "I would like to request a waiver on the portion that states she would have to submit to the whole chapter. Instead, I offer up the idea of symbolic submission in which she would only have to submit to the leader of the active chapter."

The old man in the tall hat tapped his fingers on the table in from of him as he thought out loud. "This girl desires to wait for marriage to have intercourse?"

"Yes," Declan replied.

"How do you presume you might get her to agree to this little scheme of yours?"

Declan sighed. "I do not know, but I would appreciate the opportunity to try."

The man stroked his chin with his forefinger and thumb. "I'll tell you what. I do not understand your obsession with this situation and I do not think this venture of yours will be successful. With that said, because I admire your determination and, frankly, am board with this discussion. I will give you an opportunity to sort this situation out yourself. I am thereby granting your proposal for a waiver and ruling that if she submits to you, as the current leader of the active chapter, for initiation, then you may do whatever you deem necessary to protect her, as she will be one of us."

The room broke out into a mix of protests and snorts, but Declan only noticed the knot in his chest loosening and his jumbled thoughts clearing.

"However," the man raised his voice to be heard over the commotion. "Every member of your chapter must testify to the fact that the initiation did actually occur."

"Thank you, sir." Declan nodded at the man and then turned to leave the room.

~ ~ ~

It had seemed like a long shot to get the chairman of their club to give him this chance, but since he had somehow pulled it off, Declan decided to not give up so easily when it came to convincing Destiny.

He leaned forward in his chair to explain again. "We have the ability to keep you safe no matter what the cost, but they offer complete protection only to members and their immediate families. If you became a member, my entire crew would be expected to put everything else aside to make your safety the ultimate priority. My crew and I would not only be able to skip the New York trip but would have no choice but to skip it. Unfortunately, the only way a person can become a member is if they give themselves entirely and wholly to the group. For guys it means they have to allow the group to beat them without fighting back, because, I guess, from a male perspective that shows complete submission. For girls it obviously has to be different, they give themselves wholly through… other means."

"You are telling me I have to do this with the whole group?" Destiny wrinkled her nose and rubbed her temple. "Who all is in this group? How old are some of these people?"

Declan held up his hand, palm forward, to calm her as he elaborated. "There are only four of us currently in an active chapter of the group. Technically we join as we enter high school and are in it until the age of twenty-five. After that we become alumni and serve on the advisory council. It just so happens that all of the current members are still in high school. Invitations to be admitted to the group are typically passed down from fathers to sons. None of the alumni had any sons old enough until Lex and I reached ninth grade, so the group sat in limbo for a while."

"Have girls ever been a part of this 'club' before?"

"Well, no. In fact, they have never performed the initiation process for girls ever, even though some of the families have had daughters. They just did not see it as a co-ed group."

"No kidding," spat Destiny with an eye roll. Then she began chewing on her thumbnail.

Declan ignored the comment and continued. "Nevertheless, the rules for female additions were written out in the original code of the brotherhood as a precaution for future generations." He raised his eyes to check how she was taking his explanation, but she just stared at him blankly with her mouth slightly open and then fiddled with her ring. So he continued, "We are fortunate because the council agreed that in this specific scenario, given who you are, having this form of submission played out for everyone in the group was asking too much, so they gave way on that part and decided if you at least submit to the current leader of the group it should be symbolic enough as long as every member of the active chapter testifies to the initiation actually occurring." He stopped to check her reaction again.

Destiny noticed the pause and narrowed her eyes. "Who's the current leader?"

"The leader is chosen by bloodline. My great, great, great, grandfather started this organization, and I have no older brothers so... I am." He watched as Destiny's eyes widened and her jaw dropped open. This made him nervous so he rushed forward. "If it makes you feel any better, I tried to convince the guys to lie to the board members and just say you had been initiated even though you had not, but Jesse did not want to risk expulsion from the group for dishonesty. Besides, it is really not that big of a deal if you think about it." He lifted both his hands into the air and gave a little shrug. "People do this every day just for fun. No one would hold it against you for trying to save your life."

Destiny gave her ring one quick twist, looked Declan straight in the eyes, and spoke firmly. "This *is* a big deal. In fact, for me, it is one of the biggest deals there is!" She threw one arm into the air with exasperation as she slouched back into her chair and stared at the ceiling. "I can see how the idea of doing this with me might be nothing more than a business transaction to you, because you don't believe the same way I do. But it is still wrong."

Declan's face flushed red at the accusation, and he leaned back, looked away, and spoke quietly. "It does not mean nothing to me. In fact, it means everything to me." Destiny lowered her gaze to eye him as he continued talking. "I need you to understand, Destiny. I… I care about you… strongly, and I would much rather not have to bring this idea to you. It destroys my plans for… for everything…" He looked away.

"What do you mean?" she insisted, crossing her arms.

He met her gaze and flinched. Then he swallowed and sat up straight, regaining his all-about-business demeanor. "It does not really matter. What matters most is that you are kept safe. Everything else is irrelevant if I fail at that."

Destiny mirrored his serious stature, put both hands on the armrests of her chair, and stood up to leave in order to accentuate the finality of what she was about to say. "Thank you for caring and trying to help, Declan, but I cannot accept your offer. I have to stand by what I believe is right, no matter what the consequences, and I won't sell myself, no matter the price. You have to respect my decision." With that, she was out the door.

~

Yes, she decided, *it was definitely a bad idea to go somewhere quiet. Time to head home and distract myself with a movie.*

Destiny swung her backpack over her shoulder and felt herself tilt slightly. *Wow, maybe I should just go to bed when I get home.* But by the time she reached the parking lot her head was swimming and she realized with confusion and shock, *I'm not gunna make it to my car!*

Almost instantly her legs seemed to disappear from existence, and she stumbled to the ground.

"What the… what's going on?" she tried to speak as she leaned against the tire of a nearby vehicle, but it barely came out as a mumble.

Suddenly she realized she wasn't alone. Two guys appeared on either side of her and lifted her into the air like she was sitting in a chair.

Put me down! Leave me alone! She tried to scream but instead her head just fell to the side, resting on one of their shoulders.

She fought with all of her might to stay conscious while they eased her into the door of a giant black blur. Then, as they sat her next to a guy who was waiting in the vehicle, she caught the scent of a familiar cologne. That's when she understood exactly what was going on.

"No," she barely got the word out as she urged her body to slide away from him. "Please, don't."

"It is okay," she thought she heard him say, "we are not going to hurt you, I promise." He reached over and wrapped his arms around her. "I am going to take care of you. We will go back to my place and before you know it this will all be over and you will be safe."

"Please… No…" she tried to push him away again but succeeded only in sliding her fingers across his shoulder.

"I am sorry, but I have to keep you safe," he said as he reached up and gently brushed her hair from her face.

Then the world faded away.

Chapter 5

Wednesday, October 19, 2011

PACKAGE ARRIVED SAFE at school.

Declan closed his locker and sighed in relief as he read Lex's text. He had sent Lex to make sure Destiny was kept safe as she drove to school that morning. It would be the first time she returned to school since the event. He would have gone himself, but he hadn't seen Destiny since that night and felt his emotions wouldn't allow him to be a very good bodyguard. He would have rushed up to apologize to her and ask her how she was doing, but imagining that scenario made him feel weak. She couldn't have any reason to think he was second guessing his decision or she might wonder if he could actually keep her safe. So, instead, he went to school early to wait.

Did she notice you? Declan texted back.

Don't think so. But I should warn you, she's not dressed... normal... I

guess.

What do u mean?
You'll see. Entering now.

Declan looked toward the front doors just as she walked in, and he had to bite his lower lip as a wave of emotions hit him. Usually she wore jeans and T-shirts or hoodies, but today she had on a thigh-length, low-cut red dress with knee high black boots. Her hair was curled in long ringlets which hung loose to the small of her back, and her usual backpack was replaced with a shiny black tote.

She had always looked around as she walked, smiling at everyone who returned her gaze; but today her head was held high and her eyes set straight in front of her like she was determined to not talk to anyone.

At first Declan stood entranced, unable to think of anything other than her. But then a couple of jocks in letter jackets who were leaning against their lockers let out a couple of cat calls. Destiny turned her head and shot a smile at them, sending Declan's stomach into a summersault and dropping his heart to the base of his gut. He crossed his arms on his chest and continued to watch her walk down the hall, attracting the attention of every male in the area. When he couldn't stand it any longer, he impulsively turned and slammed his fist into his locker.

"Yeah, thought you might react like that," Lex stated matter-of-factly. While Declan had been fixated on Destiny, Lex had arrived and leaned against the locker next to him.

Declan pressed both forearms against his locker and rested his forehead on his left arm, staring at the floor. "Why would she do this?"

"Come on, man," Lex said, sounding strained. "It's

not that big a deal. So she's dressing different? She looks hot!"

Declan twisted his head around, still resting it on his arm, to glare at Lex. Then he grabbed his backpack and headed to the cafeteria where they were serving breakfast for early arrivers. Destiny always grabbed a blueberry bagel and cream cheese to take to her first class, and he couldn't stand the thought of all the guys in there ogling her. He had to do something about this outfit.

As Declan entered the cafeteria he scanned the room for her and noticed she was just about to hand the cashier her money for the bagel when a guy with bleached-blond hair stepped in and paid her bill.

"You have got to be kidding me!" Declan muttered under his breath as he set out in her direction.

By the time he got through the random gatherings of high school students, she had joined a group of her girlfriends and Declan caught a little bit of their conversation as he walked over.

"We are all soooo glad you're back, Destiny," stated a girl with curly red hair as she gave Destiny a hug.

"Yes, definitely. And you look great today. How are you feeling?" added another girl as she took a hug of her own.

"Thanks, guys," Destiny responded with a half-smile. "I'm feeling pretty good, I guess. Just got to move on, you know?" She lowered her eyes to her bagel and started fiddling with its plastic wrap as the girls nodded in supportive agreement.

"Hey, Destiny," Declan interrupted while stepping between her and the redhead.

Destiny instantly tensed; then she tightened her jaw and looked up at him. "Hello, Declan," she stated as she stopped fiddling with the bagel and started squeezing it instead.

Declan paused as he glanced at her hands, then straightened his shoulders and responded formally. "It is good to see you again."

"Yes, I suppose it might be," she answered coldly as she looked back at her bagel and relaxed her grip on it.

"Of course it is, Destiny, we all missed having you here," added one of the other girls.

Declan smiled at the girl, grateful for the group situation, and then returned his gaze to Destiny.

"Well, the reason I came over here was because I could not help but notice you look a little chilly, and I wanted to offer you my jacket," Declan said as he removed his jacket and held it out to her.

The girls in the group swooned, but Destiny just shot him a quick, icy glare. The other girls didn't notice; Declan felt it like a knife. Still, he kept his composure and continued extending the jacket toward her. If there was one thing his father taught him, it was how to not let your emotions be read by others, and Declan would not falter from his decision to get Destiny covered up.

What a jerk! Destiny grumbled internally. He had her trapped. She didn't want to have to explain to her friends why she would turn down this offer, so she pasted a smile on her face and forced out a too cheery sounding, "Thank you," as she took the jacket from him and put it on.

"No problem at all." Declan sighed. The jacket hung to her knees and could almost be wrapped around her twice. *Mission accomplished!* He thought before saying, "You can use it as long as you like. I will catch you girls later. Time to head to class." He smiled and gave a small wave to them as he walked away.

"Oh. My. Gosh! How cute was that!" the redheaded girl squealed excitedly.

"Yeah, that hunk of a man is definitely crushing on you Destiny!" another girl stated.

Destiny felt as if she might throw up. "Maybe, I don't know," she said flatly.

A cacophony of protestations arose from the group.

"Come on!" the redhead said dramatically, slapping her hand on her knee. "He is so the tall, dark, and handsome type, and wealthy at that. You should go for it," she added firmly while crossing her arms.

Destiny grimaced but hoped it came across as a hesitant smile.

The girl who stood to her left put her hand on Destiny's shoulder as she came to her defense. "Maybe she's not ready yet girls, give her some time to rehabilitate or whatever. Besides, she's been friends with Declan like forever; he will wait 'till she's ready."

The group grew somber as they nodded in realization and agreement. Then the two-minute warning bell rang and they said their goodbyes and dispersed.

Destiny paused outside her classroom. *He* was going to be in there, and she had dreaded this moment since she woke up in the hospital. But she had already seen him before she had expected to this morning and made it through fine. In a way he had done her a favor by catching her off-guard. Sitting next to him in class shouldn't be too tough now. She wouldn't even need to talk to him. All she had to do was ignore him. With a deep breath she headed through the door and sat in her seat just before the tardy bell sounded.

He was sitting one desk ahead of her to her right. As she started unwrapping her mutilated bagel she felt his gaze on her, so she glanced up. Sure enough, Declan was turned slightly and looking over his shoulder at her, but when she caught his eye he quickly turned away.

That's right, selfish jerk-face! She felt a small rush of empowerment flow through her, raising her confidence.

Unfortunately, as class waned on, that feeling dwindled as she realized that the jacket she was wearing smelled of Declan's cologne. Her stomach began to churn as images flashed across her memory: jet black sheets, a wooden headboard, her tennis shoes lying on the floor across the room…

I have to get rid of this thing! She thought desperately. Fortunately, she had an idea and raised her hand.

"Yes, Destiny?" her English Literature teacher called on her.

"Sorry, ma'am. May I go to the restroom?"

"Of course," the teacher replied. "Don't forget to grab the hall pass."

Destiny exhaled slowly. As a rule, this teacher never let anyone leave during a lecture, but Destiny's recent situation probably explained the extra leniency.

Declan turned to watch her grab the hall pass and head out the door. His brows furrowed in obvious concern, but that just made Destiny's stomach churn more, so she quickened her pace.

As soon as she stood alone in the girl's restroom she whipped off the jacket and threw it over a stall door. Then she hustled over to the sink and started scrubbing her arms to get rid of the smell.

She used to like Declan's cologne. In fact, she had helped him choose it. But that seemed like ages ago, and now the smell had become her enemy as it fought her will power and bombarded her psyche.

Once her arms were sufficiently washed, she rested her hands firmly on the sink and stared at her reflection in the mirror. She looked like a stranger. The clothes she was wearing were definitely inappropriate; but that was precisely why she had chosen them. She reasoned that if she was defiled and dirty anyway, she might as well enjoy some attention from boys in a way she had control over.

No sense holding back now, she thought as tears threatened to squeeze out. But, instead of breaking down, she breathed deep and stood taller. She wasn't powerless. Maybe she couldn't turn Declan and his crew in, but she could make him squirm.

Turning sideways as she looked into the mirror, she rolled her shoulders back and smiled firmly before walking out of the bathroom, leaving the jacket behind.

Declan tapped his index finger nervously on his desk and glanced at the clock again. She had only been gone ten minutes but each minute felt like a lifetime; what if they had gotten her? *They wouldn't dare kidnap someone on school grounds with so many people around… then again…*

He had swung his legs into the aisle and was about to stand up to go check on her when she returned.

Relief flooded Declan's body, but it deserted him quickly and was replaced with a slightly-less-urgent concern as he noticed the guy sitting next to him shift to get a better look at her.

Why isn't she wearing my jacket?

He shot her a quizzical look, but she shrugged it off and ignored him. He tore a piece of paper from his notebook and wrote "Jacket?" on it. Then he waited for the teacher to turn her back and slipped it onto Destiny's desk.

Destiny glanced down at the paper, put on a feigned

expression of confusion, then shock, and wrote back, "Oops, I think I forgot it in the bathroom." Then she returned it to Declan just as stealthily.

After reading her response he glanced at her. She raised her eyebrows, curled her lips into a pressed half smile, and shrugged her shoulders.

He sighed and turned away. She was definitely angry with him. *I was foolish to expect anything else.* He rested his forehead in his hand. *What now?*

Chapter 6

DESTINY STOOD BY THE row of windows and stared out at the parking lot. After she had ditched the jacket the rest of her first day back at school had gone fairly well. Declan had avoided eye contact, and she had been able to free her mind to pay attention to her classes. The temporary return to normalcy had convinced her to try staying after school to tutor a freshman in algebra, just like she used to do on Wednesdays. However, now that the session was over and she was standing alone in the room, she was starting to think it had been a mistake.

From the classroom she had a good view of her car, which was located toward the front of the parking lot; but the clock showed the time to be slightly after four and the parking lot looked vacant.

It's still daylight Destiny. You don't have anything to worry about. She was trying to console herself, but her pulse continued to race. After all, it was daylight the first time her life was threatened a little over three weeks earlier when she had decided to go for a walk.

Saturday, September 24, 2011

It was the perfect weather for walking, warm enough to need only a hoody instead of a winter coat, and Destiny had decided to take advantage of it.

The wind picked up as she neared a small park a few blocks from her house, and she began to consider heading home before it got too cold when a guy with a cheap plastic monkey mask jumped out from behind a bush and confronted her.

"Hello there, girly. How would you like to come on a little trip with me?" he asked in a deep gravelly voice.

"Uh." Destiny stifled a chuckle at the peculiarity of his mask, but the hair on the back of her neck stood on end; so, she stuck her hand into her pocket to grip the bottle of pepper spray her father had insisted she carry. Then she stated, "No thanks," as she began to turn away from him toward home, only to find two more monkey-masked guys behind her.

The second she realized she was surrounded, she sent pepper spray flying through the eyeholes of the two monkey masks who had snuck up behind her. As they cried out in shock, she shoved her way past them and took off full-sprint toward home, but she wasn't fast enough.

The first man who had surprised her from the bushes wasn't in the vicinity of the spray and was a faster runner than Destiny. She had made it only a few yards when she felt herself being shoved sideways.

As she hit the ground she didn't fight the momentum of the shove, allowing herself to roll over a couple of times to get as far away from him as possible before coming to a stop on her back in the middle of the road that ran along the outside of the park. She quickly sat up. The masked man was laughing and slowly walking toward her.

"You thought you could escape? We can't let you go that easily. Revenge is too sweet to let it get away from us, especially when it's close enough to taste."

"Revenge?" Destiny asked, struggling to catch her breath as she tried to stand up. A sharp pain screamed through her ankle, and she dropped back to the ground. *Come on Destiny, focus. Ignore the pain!* "Why revenge? How?" she gasped.

"A life for a life, of course." He glanced toward his comrades as they stumbled in their direction. "A shame you're so pretty, but we have to hit them where it hurts the most," he explained as he reached down to grab her arm. She slapped it away.

"Don't touch me," Destiny said calmly.

The man in the mask laughed. "You don't sound scared. Bravery is hard to come by." He shrugged. "Another shame." The other two monkeys arrived at his side. "Grab her and let's get out of here," he commanded them.

But just as they started pulling her to her feet, a police car came speeding around the corner with sirens wailing.

The three guys jumped. "Never mind, leave her. Let's go!" the leader hollered and then they took off running. "We will be back for you later!" he yelled over his shoulder as they disappeared into the bushes and trees of the park.

Destiny watched them run off, her mind reeling with questions. *Why would they want revenge on me? ...on someone who cares about me? But who? And why?*

The police car came to a screeching halt right next to her.

"Destiny! Are you all right?"

"Dad? Dad!" She didn't know why she was so surprised. After all, she knew her dad was working that evening. "Yeah, I'm okay, I might have twisted my ankle though," she explained.

"I was worried I wouldn't get to you in time," he blurted as he hurried over to help her up. "When your mother said you had gone for a walk, I panicked."

"Wha… why?" She went for walks all the time; why would this time be any different? "I don't understand what's going on." Mr. Ackerman helped her into the passenger seat of his police car.

"Just let me get you home. I'll explain everything once you are safe and we have some ice on that ankle."

Wednesday, October 19, 2011

Destiny shook her head back and forth to bring herself back to reality. *Well it's not getting any earlier. Better I leave now rather than later. Time to go home. No big deal.* After wiggling her arms to loosen them up she reached into her backpack to grab her keys and then turned around to find herself face to face with a striped blue tie.

Destiny gasped and dropped her keys.

"Whoa, calm down," the man said as he clasped her shoulders in his hands.

Destiny looked up and her heart began to slow. "Lex," she gasped, "why are you here?"

"To protect you, duh." He let go of her shoulders and knelt down to swipe up her keys. "You know that was part of the deal."

Destiny's features went stone cold. "A deal I did *not* want any part of," she spat out. "Give me my keys."

Lex released a low whistle and rolled his eyes. "Afraid

I can't do that. My job is to get you safely home." He leaned against one of the desks, twirling the keys around his fingers. "Normally I would just watch from a distance driving behind you in my own car, but this note was found taped to the inside of your locker." He stealthily reached into his jacket pocket and pulled out a piece of folded paper. Then he held it out to her, seeming disinterested.

Destiny reluctantly took the paper from him and unfolded it to find nothing but a simple drawing of a monkey head. A chill ran up her spine, but her pride was stronger, so she pursed her lips together and fixed her eyes on Lex.

"I don't want your help," she stated firmly.

Lex fixed his stare right back at her, held it for a few seconds as if trying to read her, and then shrugged. "It doesn't matter." He stood up and stepped closer to her so she had to tilt her head up to maintain her glare. "You should understand by now that whether you want our help or not, we are going to be giving it to you in whatever ways we can. Now, you can either follow me out the back exit of this school to my limo where the rest of the crew is waiting and let us drive you home; *or* I will carry you out the back door of this school to my limo where the rest of the crew is waiting and we will drive you home."

Destiny swallowed, lowered her eyes, and took a step back. "Fine, I'll come," she said reluctantly. "Just don't touch me."

Lex raised an eyebrow and shrugged again. "Wouldn't dream of it. Now let's go."

Destiny swung her backpack over her shoulder and began following him. "Wait, how did you get into my locker, and how am I going to get my car home?"

Lex glanced over his shoulder at her but kept walking.

"You gave Declan your locker combo last month, and we will have Johnny drop your car at your house."

"So, you guys just decided you had the right to search my locker?" Destiny asked accusingly.

"Yes, of course," he stated matter-of-factly.

She sighed.

"Here we are." Lex held the door open to the lesser used exit of the school. "After you," he stated formally as he motioned with his arm for her to go through the door.

The limo's engine was running silently, parked right outside. It was even pulled halfway onto the sidewalk.

"Ugh, you guys are so lame," she exclaimed as Lex rushed ahead to open the door of the limo for her.

"It's called chivalry; you used to like it," Lex responded with a wry smile.

"Yeah, but now it reminds me of you," Destiny said sourly, causing Lex to grab his chest with his hand, faking a pain in his heart.

Destiny let out a snort as she ducked into the limo only to be faced with three more boys in suits, including Declan.

"I see you retrieved your jacket," she said flatly as she made her way to a seat as far away from Declan as possible.

Declan glanced at her for a second and then looked away, gazing out the window.

"Some nice, *civilized* ladies went in and grabbed it for us," said Lex as he climbed into the car behind her. Then he tossed her car keys to Johnny.

Johnny was the quietest of the group and also significantly the largest when it came to shoulder width and muscle definition. He glanced at Destiny as he caught the keys and smiled kindly. Then he nodded at Lex as he lumbered out of the limo, closing the door behind him. Destiny watched him through the window as they pulled away and realized that, out of the group, she probably hated Johnny the least.

"Nice dress Destiny, did your mother give it to you?"

Destiny looked to her left. The snide remark had come from Jesse. He was a shorter guy about Destiny's height, with mixed features that made one assume he was part Asian. Yet both of his "birth" parents where German. She had always suspected an unfaithful wife to be the cause of this, but Destiny had never brought it up before. It just seemed like too mean a thing for her to mention. But, times had changed.

"Nice eyes, Jesse. Did your father give them to you?" She shot back.

At first silence engulfed the air, but slowly Jesse's eyes narrowed, and he clenched his fist. Then Lex broke into boisterous laughter while slapping his knee, and Declan turned his eyes away from the window to stare at Destiny with disbelief. Destiny just stared right back, fixing him with a firm and unwavering glare.

Declan crossed his arms across his chest and slouched back in his chair, still staring at Destiny. "Really, though," he stated, "you should be more careful about what you wear. You do not want to attract the wrong type of guy."

"Who said anything about the wrong guy? I'm thinking more of one specific one." Destiny couldn't believe herself, she didn't even really know what she was talking about, but the idea of Declan lecturing her, thinking he had any power over her, was more than she could stand.

Declan's face flushed red as he sat up quickly and leaned forward. "What guy?" he questioned too urgently.

"That's really not any of your concern." It was now Destiny's turn to cross her arms and stare out the window. Declan just kept eyeing her up and down.

"I'll bet you it's that one from gym class," Lex threw his voice in. "You know, that nerd who's too tall for correct balance."

Again, Lex took a turn getting the glare. It seemed Destiny had used her glare more this one day than the rest of her life combined. "That guy's name is Darren, and he happens to be very sweet."

Lex responded with a guffaw followed by, "Oh, I'm sorry. I forgot he's a real cutie-pie."

Declan just kept eyeing Destiny with such burning intensity that she studiously avoided him and kept glaring at Lex for the next few minutes, while Jesse sat grumbling in his seat. Eventually, Declan broke the silence with a voice slightly louder than a whisper.

"You just have to be careful, Destiny. People are not always what they seem. You do not know much about this guy at all. For all you know he could…" he trailed off, not wanting to continue the thought.

"He could what?" she replied matching his quiet even tone. "He could masquerade as my friend and then one day steal one of my most precious possessions from me?"

Declan's jaw dropped slightly as he struggled to find words. "I… I just… wanted to… I thought… I mean, I am…"

The fire rose up within Destiny's chest, too much to hold in, and tears sprang from her eyes as her voice began to rise. "You're what, Declan! You're sorry? You couldn't possibly be sorry, because you obviously don't even realize what you have done to me!"

This was the first time since they were kids she had

ever seen Declan completely lose his composure as he desperately searched for the ability to defend himself. "No! I was just protecting you, this was the only way I could know you would stay safe! I made the decision that needed to be made for your benefit!" He blinked a thin layer of tears away.

Lex held his eyes wide open as he quickly switched his focus back and forth between the two of them, completely hooked to the drama. Even Jesse had lost interest in his own self-pity as he watched this new conversation unfold.

"Don't even go there, Declan! I made it clear this was not what I wanted, but you ignored my desires entirely!" Destiny paused for a breath. "If you cared about me, you would have respected my decision!"

Declan fell to his knees in the middle of the limo as he leaned toward her to make his point. "But you were wrong, Destiny! Your decision was wrong. They would have killed you! And I would not have been able to do anything about it." His voice tapered off and his eyes dropped to the floor in front of him. "I could not live with myself if anything happened to you."

Destiny was certain she would spontaneously combust any moment now, so she clenched her teeth for a second before she responded, and when she did it was barely audible. "They could not have done anything worse to me than what you did." With that, tears began to pour from her eyes, and she resigned herself to staring out the window again as she wiped the tears away.

Declan knelt in silence for a while just staring at her, eyes filled with pain, as he realized her suffering. Inside he felt his entire world start to slip away, but he refused to give it up just yet. Eventually she would have to understand.

"Well," Lex broke the silence, "I hate to destroy this party, but we are almost to your house, and there is some business that needs to be discussed."

"Like what?" Destiny sniffled out coldly as she turned toward Lex. Declan continued to stare at her pleadingly, but she refused to acknowledge him.

"The guys and I are going to be setting up rotating shifts for stakeouts to watch you when you're home," Lex explained in a business tone, "but it's obvious we would be much better at guarding you if we could be near you. So, you need to come up with a reason your parents will accept for us to be chillin' at your house all the time."

Destiny let out a small snort. "You want me to convince my parents to let you guys practically live with us?"

"Yes, of course," Lex stated. "You have until tomorrow."

"What could I possibly say to make that not seem odd?" Destiny's mind raced in circles, flustered. "Boys are kind of the last thing my parents want me to be around right now."

"You will think of something," said Declan. He had regained composer and reclaimed his seat, face void of any emotion and eyes straight ahead and calm.

Destiny eyed him suspiciously. "Fine," she responded.

"Yes, you will," added Lex as they pulled up in front of her house. "Shall I walk you to the door your highness?"

"Do I have a choice?" she asked.

"Nope." Lex swung the door open and stood, waiting for her to exit.

As Destiny left the limo she spared one more glance at Declan, but he continued to stare straight ahead.

Normally, having a conversation where she spoke so harshly would have left her feeling terrible, but as she entered the safety of her home, it surprised Destiny to realize she felt nothing but tired.

Chapter 7

AS SOON AS SHE WALKED through her front door, Destiny reset the security alarm and ran upstairs to her room to change her clothes. She expected her parents to be home from work any minute, and she didn't want them to see what she was wearing.

"Destiny!" Sure enough just as she pulled a T-shirt over her head she heard her parents come in and her mom call for her. It always amazed her how they worked at different places, her father a police officer and her mother an EMT, yet they seemed to arrive home at the exact same time every day.

"Yes, Mom, coming," she yelled back as she headed down the stairs.

They both greeted her at the bottom of the staircase.

"How was your first day back at school?" Mrs. Ackerman looked at her with concern as she pulled her into a hug.

"It went pretty well," Destiny answered, "better than I expected to be honest."

"When did you get home?" her dad asked as he, too, hugged her.

"Just a few minutes ago. I stayed after to tutor algebra."

"Destiny," Mr. Ackerman's voice took on a new level of seriousness, "I'm not sure that was a good idea. I let you go to school because while you are there you are surrounded by people, but staying after when everyone's gone is reckless."

Destiny sighed as she walked into the kitchen to get a drink of water. "I know Dad, I agree, it was probably a mistake."

She looked out the window into the backyard as she filled up her cup from the sink. That's when it hit her—the perfect excuse for the guys to be spending time at her house, and one that she might actually get some enjoyment from.

"I just wanted things to feel normal again," she continued, "but it was too soon. I won't do it again."

Mr. Ackerman put his arm around her shoulders. "Good. At least until we get this gang behind bars. The department seems certain the attack on you last Friday was the worst they intend. But, I'm still worried it might not have been them, or even if it was them it may have just been a mean trick of suspense to hurt us worse and they will come back for more." He paused as his voice caught in his throat. "I'm just so sorry this is happening. It's all my fault."

Destiny turned to her father and hugged him again. "Dad, you didn't do anything wrong. You saved the life of a little boy when you shot that man who was threatening him. Whatever the stupid gang he belonged to does because of it is not your fault. It's their choice. They are the only ones to blame for their actions."

Her dad smiled at her. "How did you get so smart and brave?"

"She learned it from her father," Mrs. Ackerman chimed in as she patted him on the back.

Destiny nodded her head and chuckled. "Most definitely," she agreed. "But there is something I should show you. Just don't freak out too much. I'm not certain what it means yet. It was taped to the inside of my locker." She spoke tentatively as she handed him the paper Lex had found.

Mr. Ackerman opened it and his eyes grew dark as he took in the monkey picture. "I'm calling the department; they need to know about this."

Destiny and her mother watched as he urgently explained to his boss what was found. After he finished he simply said, "Yes, sir," nodded his head and hung up.

"What did he say?" Destiny inquired.

"He was pretty upset, and rightfully so. This means they have been in your school, and that's bad news for everybody, not just us. So, they will be sending more cars to patrol your school and are upping the amount of officers who are already walking the halls. As for what it means for you personally, we don't really know. He thinks it could be a calling card, something criminals leave after a crime to mark it as theirs. If that's the case, it means they are responsible for what happened to you last Friday night. But if it's not a calling card, then it's a threat, and I refuse to take any more chances. So, he said they would also be sending a patrol car to keep an eye on the house overnight, and I'm not letting you go anywhere alone."

"Okay," was all Destiny could think of as a response. She hated lying to her parents, but she felt she had no choice in this situation. If she wanted to have the best possible odds to keep herself and her family safe she could not tell them she knew the gang wasn't to blame for Friday night. As upset as she was at Declan right now, the connections he had could be very useful. His father was the governor and on the advisory council for this club of his. Therefore, he was on her side now, and, also, doing whatever he could to put a stop to this gang. *Besides,* she reasoned with herself, *the police not knowing doesn't hurt the investigation any. They are still going to treat things as if we are in danger. If anything, it gives them a stronger desire to catch these guys.*

"Now that that's settled," Mrs. Ackerman interrupted her thoughts, "I have a few other questions. Where's your car and how did you get home?"

"Oh," Destiny started. *I almost forgot. Well I guess this is my chance to do my homework.* "About that, do you remember my friend Declan?" Destiny fought a grimace as she worked out the word *friend.*

"Yes, of course, the governor's son who's in love with you," her mom answered.

"Mom!" Destiny couldn't contain herself. "He's not… please don't say that."

Mrs. Ackerman mistook Destiny's reaction for modesty. "Okay, okay, I'm sorry." She smiled, took a step back and waved her hands in the air in mock defense. "Please continue with your explanation."

Destiny took a couple breaths to calm herself and shook her head in disbelief before continuing. "Anyway, he found out about that monkey picture in my locker and insisted on giving me a ride home. He promised to drop my car off later tonight."

"Wow," Mr. Ackerman chimed in, "that was really nice of him. Remind me to thank him next time I see him."

"Yes," her mom added, "it's good to know someone at school cares about you and is looking out for you." She said with finger quotes around "cares".

Destiny felt bile rising in her throat and swallowed it back down. She had to act normal. "Yeah, well, I've got a way you guys can thank him."

"Really, what's that?" asked Mr. Ackerman.

"He and three of his friends are in a landscaping class at school." A smile broke out on Destiny's face as she pictured them getting dirt on their suits. "For their final exam their teacher let the class split into groups, so naturally they picked each other, and they have to present to him a yard that they have actually landscaped themselves. Declan has been really worried about it because they haven't been able to find anyone willing to let high school boys touch their yards. After all, they live in fancy-pants neighborhoods and everyone there already has their yards landscaped. So, it would really relieve him of a lot of stress if you guys let them use our backyard. The school funds all the expenses and everything. It would be like a free yard makeover."

Destiny watched as excitement grew on her mother's face. Their backyard had been the bane of their existence for a while, because no one in the family really cared for yard work. As a result, it had become overrun with weeds, and Destiny knew her mother would love for that mess to be remedied.

Mr. Ackerman laughed. "You mean to tell me, the way we can thank this boy for driving our daughter home safely is to allow him to remodel our backyard without charging us for his work?"

"Yes." Destiny grinned. "You would have to be okay with them spending a lot of time here. It will probably take the rest of the semester to finish the work with everything else they have to do, especially since they are only amateur landscapers."

"Well, to be honest, that might be a bonus," he reasoned. "Having all those boys over all the time would only make the house safer for you." He shrugged his shoulders and smiled. "I really have no reason to say no."

"Great!" Destiny said as she gave a little hop and her mom clapped her hands together. "Can I have them come over tomorrow after school to scope out the yard?"

"The sooner the better," Mr. Ackerman answered.

"Awesome, I can't wait to let them know. Thanks, you guys." And once again Destiny passed out hugs.

That night Destiny went to bed with a smile on her face as she thought about how much those guys were going to "love" this plan.

Chapter 8

Thursday, October 20, 2011

"DESTINY, WHAT…" Lex didn't get to finish his sentence, because the second he began talking from behind her, Destiny spun around and punched him in the gut.

"Oh, it's you," she said calmly as he grabbed his stomach and stumbled backwards a couple of steps. She watched as Declan, who had been standing next to Lex reached out to steady him. "Dang, I got the wrong guy," she added as she turned around to close her locker.

Declan just looked at her, expressionless as he patted Lex on the back.

"Got to remember not to startle you," Lex gasped out. "Wow, police officer father taught you how to pack a punch."

Destiny smiled inwardly. She had known they were there from the second they walked up, but she thought she would take advantage of the opportunity to slug one of them.

"Anyway," Lex added as he straightened his tie, "do you have information for us? Some sort of plan that will allow us to hang at your place indefinitely?"

This time Destiny allowed the smile to manifest itself outwardly as she began walking toward her classroom with them following. "Yes, I do. In fact, I have the perfect plan. My parents even approved of you guys coming over after school today to get started on it."

"Really?" Declan questioned. He seemed surprised and suspicious at the same time.

"Tell us," Lex insisted with arms extended and raised slightly.

"Okay, I will." Destiny whirled around to face them, stopping them awkwardly in their tracks. "I told them you guys would be landscaping our back yard as an assignment for your landscaping class."

"What? We aren't in a landscaping class," Lex said. He looked confused, but Declan seemed to understand almost instantly and let out a sigh.

Destiny crossed her arms and tilted her head to the side. "You are now," she stated. "You need to complete an actual landscaping project for your final grade. So, I convinced my parents to allow you to use our backyard." She turned around again to continue walking but still talked to them over her shoulder. "Oh, and I told them they wouldn't have to pay a dime because it's a school project and the school would fund it, but I'm sure you guys can take care of that money issue, no problem." She waved them off as she entered her classroom and added, "See you later."

Declan and Lex stopped in the middle of the hallway to watch her walk through the door. Then Lex turned toward Declan, a you've-got-to-be-kidding-me expression on his face. Declan simply gave him a wry smile in return.

September 4, 2009

After exiting the vehicle, Declan spun around to watch her climb out behind him. The look on her face was priceless as she took in the scenery.

"Wow!" Destiny said, turning to Declan with a smile that made the world seem brighter. "Thanks for asking me to come along."

Declan smiled back as they stepped to the side to allow the rest of the guys and their dates to get out of the limo as well.

Lex, Jesse, and Johnny had practically begged Declan to allow them to take their girlfriends to his mother's apple orchard, but Declan had been hesitant. It was the beginning of his sophomore year of high school and Declan was the only one in their group without a girlfriend because the only girl he wanted to date didn't date.

"Come on, man," Lex had begged, "it's the perfect time of year for this. The girls are going to love it."

"I just do not want to be the…" Declan paused to count, "… seventh wheel, you know?"

"Then ask some girl to come with us; it doesn't really matter who," Jesse chimed in.

Declan, annoyed, turned toward Jesse. "You know I cannot do that. I do not want just any girl."

Johnny placed his hand on Declan's shoulder. "Well then, ask *her* to come," he added. "It doesn't have to be a date, just two friends hanging out."

So, Declan had done just that. He had asked Destiny to come with him as a friend, and she had said yes.

"This place really is beautiful," Destiny said as she strolled with Declan through the rows of trees. The rest of the group had split into couples and dispersed. "Why does your father own an apple orchard?"

"Technically it is my mother's. My father bought it for her," Declan stated.

"That actually sounds pretty romantic of him," she said with a hint of surprise in her voice.

Declan chuckled. "Not really. It was more of an apology gift than a romantic gift."

Destiny paused in her walking and turned to him. "What do you mean?"

Declan sighed as he reached up to pull a few leaves from a tree. "When I was about ten years old my mother caught my father cheating on her. My father probably could not care less about how she felt, but he could not have her divorcing him and running around telling the press about it. That would give him a bad image. So, he decided to buy an apple orchard to subdue her. It worked; they are still unhappily married."

"That sucks. I'm sorry you had to go through that, Declan."

She seemed genuinely concerned, and it brought a smile to his face. Of course, she was concerned; she was always caring, that was one of the many things he liked about her.

"Do not worry about it." He responded as he tossed a couple of leaves into her hair. She giggled as she brushed them off. "Besides, it was not all bad, he did at least buy her an orchard full of her favorite type of apple instead of one she did not care for."

"What type is that?" Destiny asked as she pulled the last leaf out of her hair and tossed it back at him, which he artfully dodged.

"The Honeycrisp," he stated.

"Oh yeah, that type is pretty good, but it's not my favorite."

"Really?" Declan asked. "What is your favorite then?"

"The Spartan, naturally," she said with a playful smile, "reminds me of the movie *300*." Then she added with a shrug, "Plus they taste pretty good."

Declan laughed. "That would be your reasoning, wouldn't it." He reached up and plucked an apple from a tree then held it out to her while saying in a deep, gravelly voice, "Immortality, take it! It's yours!"

Destiny couldn't contain herself and fell to her knees in laughter.

"Wow, I didn't think it was that funny," Declan stated, but he couldn't resist laughing some himself. Her laughter was the contagious type.

"Sorry, it's… it's just that…" she struggled to control her laughter. "You made me picture the Spartans in suit jackets on the battlefield." She laughed again before continuing, "Plus… that seemed more like a scene from the Garden of Eden than from *300*."

Declan began chuckling himself. "Yeah, I suppose it might." After a few seconds he sat down next to her on the grass and added, "Speaking of the Garden of Eden, I actually have a question for you about it."

Destiny brought her laughter under control and looked at him, eyes still sparkling. "What's your question?"

"It is just that, I have always kind of wondered—if God knew Adam and Eve would disobey Him and destroy everything, why did He still decide to create them?"

Destiny smiled at him. "That's a good question," she said. "If God had wanted He could have even made them incapable of choosing against Him, but He didn't."

"Why didn't He?" Declan looked concerned.

"Well, you would like to get married someday, right?" she asked.

Declan's chest tightened, hearing that question come from her caught him off-guard, and he had to fight back the flush that rushed to his face. "Yes, of course," he answered quickly to get her to continue.

"And I'm assuming you would want your wife to love you, right?"

Declan nodded.

"So, to guarantee her love, you could choose to buy a robot for a wife and have her programmed to love you no matter what. Does that sound appealing to you?"

"Definitely not," Declan answered, a little confused.

She smiled again. "Do you see why that is? It's because love isn't really love if the person does not have the ability to choose against it. Love cannot be forced if it is going to mean anything. It has to be given by her free will."

Declan stared off into the distance while he thought about it. "Yeah, I understand that."

"Well, it's the same with God. He created people because He wanted a relationship with us, but a forced relationship would mean nothing. We have to be able to choose. So, that's why He gave us free will. Then, when Adam and Eve chose to act against God's will. They inherited a nature which desires to sin instead of following God's instructions. This caused all of their descendants to be born with the same sin nature. Fortunately for us, God still loved us enough to die on the cross to pay for that nature and its consequences. In other words, He made a way for us to still be able to choose to have a relationship with Him and love Him, despite our mistakes. Giving us the ability to choose was the only way He could have true love from any of us."

"But a lot of people do not choose Him." Declan furrowed his brow.

"Yes, and that upsets God more than we can imagine. But, some people do choose Him, and some of us is better than none of us—or even a whole bunch of robots that are forced to choose Him. Does that make sense?"

Declan looked at Destiny. Her eyes were wide and bright; he couldn't help but smile again.

"It does make sense," he answered. "You always know exactly what to say, don't you?"

"Only sometimes," she said with a light laugh, pulling a handful of grass from the ground and placing it on top of his head. She stood and ran further into the orchard.

Declan immediately jumped up and chased her down, wrapping his arm around her waist to hold her still while he rubbed some grass into her hair. She giggled and playfully pushed him away, then leaned against a tree branch to once again clear her hair of a plant invasion. Declan watched her, smiling as he pulled himself up to sit on a branch in front of her.

"I have another question," he said.

"Yes?" Destiny raised her eyes to meet his as she ran her fingers through her hair.

"Why is it someone as beautiful as you has decided to stay single?" He watched, entranced, as color rose to her cheeks and she giggled awkwardly.

"I'm only a sophomore," she explained. "Dating is supposed to be something people do when they are looking for someone to marry. I don't plan to get married at least until I'm out of high school. So, why would I date?"

"For fun, of course," Declan stated, swinging his legs back and forth.

Destiny smiled. "It wouldn't be very fun in the end. A dating relationship now would be pretty much guaranteed to end in a break-up. It's like saying, 'Hi, I like you, let's spend all our time together so that someday we can hate each other and never want to see each other again'."

She paused as she tried and failed to swing herself up onto the branch next to Declan. He reached down and helped pull her up. Once she was safely in place next to him, she continued.

"Anyway, this way I get to enjoy spending time with guys as friends, like you." She patted him on the shoulder. "I'd hate to destroy our friendship just for a sure-to-fail attempt at love and then have to avoid you in the hallways. That would suck," she said with a grimace.

Declan gave one quick laugh and put his arm around her to give her a half hug. "That *would* suck."

Just then Jesse and his date walked by their tree and Jesse started up, annoyingly chanting, "Declan and Destiny sitting in a tree…"

Declan flushed pink as he removed his arm from Destiny's shoulder, but she just reached up to grab a couple of apples and handed one to him. Then with a mischievous grin she yelled out, "Spartans!" and let her apple fly toward Jesse.

Chapter 9

Saturday, April 21, 2011

"LISTEN UP ALL YOU YOUNG men out there. This next slow jam is the perfect opportunity for you to pull a lovely young lady close to you, so don't mess it up, and get to dancing!" the disk jockey exclaimed right before turning up the music to the next song.

Declan was standing to the right side of the dance floor, next to the punch bowl, with his hands in his suit pockets as melodic lyrics boomed in his ears. A female in a blue, sequined, mermaid-cut dress smiled at him as she grabbed a glass and took a slow sip; but he barely noticed because he was preoccupied with scanning the room for Destiny.

It was their junior prom, and Declan had come alone. Not because no one was willing to come with him; in fact, three girls had asked him to take them to prom, but he had politely refused. He had planned to ask Destiny to go with him. Unfortunately, he had chickened out every time the subject came up—a fact he was quite ashamed of and claimed to his friends never happened. As far as they were concerned he had heard she was planning to go with a group of girls who didn't have prom dates, and he didn't want to interfere with her plans. So, here he was; alone at prom, and, according to the DJ, this was his chance to dance with Destiny at least once.

It didn't take him long to find her. She was wearing a bright pink dress, had sprayed glitter into her hair, and had clipped a lime green flower just above and behind her left ear. She was standing across the dance floor, talking and laughing with two other girls. Declan couldn't help but smile when he noticed she was barefoot. She never enjoyed wearing high heels and must have ditched her shoes the second she got inside.

Well, this is my chance, he thought as he took a deep breath. *Just go ask her to dance.* He began making his way over to her.

When he was about five feet away she seemed to realize he was coming and turned toward him, smiling and making eye contact. This stopped him right in his tracks as he took in every little detail of her face. Even her eyelashes were glittery, and her lipstick was a deep purple that seemed to shimmer when she smiled. Declan forgot to breathe.

Destiny's smile twitched as she gave him a look that said, "what's the matter?" and let out a nervous little chuckle before dropping her eyes to the ground.

Wow... Was all Declan could think as he stood there transfixed, but then his stupor was broken as a guy about his same height and slightly stockier bumped into his shoulder.

"Whoa, sorry man," the guy said as he pointed his thumb over his own shoulder in the direction he headed, "just squeezing through."

Declan nodded at him in acknowledgement and turned his focus back to Destiny. Unfortunately, her focus had been turned away and she was talking to a guy whom Declan knew to be named Stan.

"Hey, Destiny," Stan was saying, "you look absolutely gorgeous tonight! Your date is one lucky guy."

"Oh," she responded with a little laugh as she reached behind her back with her right hand and twirled a strand of hair between her fingers. "Thank you, but I don't really have a date tonight. Just came with some friends."

Declan glared as he watched the smile on Stan's face grow. "Wow!" Stan said. "Guess it's my lucky day." Destiny laughed nervously and gave a quick glance toward Declan.

Hey, Stan, Declan thought, *she is not interested. Just leave now.*

"May I have this dance then, lovely lady?" Stan asked with a flourish, holding his hand out to her and bowing his head slightly.

"Oh," Destiny said again as she covered her mouth with her hand. "I…" Then, she unmistakably looked directly at Declan and paused.

Declan's jaw dropped slightly. He wasn't sure what to do, and instead of stepping in and grabbing her hand himself—like he wanted to—he simply looked away as if he didn't notice what was happening.

Destiny furrowed her eyebrows at him then turned back to Stan and smiled. "Yes, I do think I would enjoy a dance with you." She placed her hand in his. He immediately twirled her in a circle, causing a surprised gasp trailed by laughter to escape her lips.

"Well, that was weird," Lex's voice intruded, causing Declan to grimace and sigh.

"Where is your date, Lex?"

"I think she's trying to spike the punch to impress me," Lex said with a smirk. "But, I'm not so easily wooed, so she's in for a disappointment. Kinda like you," he added with a "Hah!"

Declan clasped his hands behind his back and checked his poker face for kinks before responding, "I do not know what you are talking about."

"Come on, man! I totally noticed that weird mojo eye-contact thing you and Destiny were sharing. You had her right in your grasp, but the next thing I saw was lover boy over there whisking her away and you just watching it happen, like a total tool. What's up, man?"

"It is just one dance, Lex."

"Yeah, one dance. Okay, let's watch this one dance. Where's the happy couple?" Lex scanned the dance floor until he found them. "There," he said pointing at them. "Oh, how cute! Look, he's even got a pink tie to match her dress. Awww… it's like they planned it!"

Declan stood as still as a statue, not wanting to give Lex any satisfaction by reacting.

"Would you look at that, his hand is resting quite nicely on her hip there. I wonder how many guys she has let get that close?" He tapped his chin and eyed Declan. "I'm guessing not you; no, you probably haven't even held her hand for longer than a few seconds… except maybe when you were kids." Declan swallowed and blinked a couple of times. "Yeah, that's what I thought. Anyway, back to the show. Oh, look! He's twirling her and… oh… oh no, a strand of her hair is stuck to her face, but she doesn't seem to mind; still smiling and laughing away. Maybe you should go help her and pull that out of her way since all of their hands seem to be busy." Declan let out an irritated grunt and rolled his eyes. "Careful there, bud," said Lex, "your face is getting a little rosy. Perhaps you should get a glass of water or something."

"Is there a point to this?" Declan asked irritably.

"Is there a point to this?" Lex mimicked then slapped Declan on the back. "Yes! Of course there is a point to this. The point is you need to stop being a pansy and start making some moves. A girl like that is not going to be single forever!"

"What am I supposed to do?" Declan sounded exasperated, "she does not date."

"That makes no difference in that it should be you out on that dance floor with her instead of that loser. You need to take every chance you can get to be close to her so that when she is ready to date you are the first and, ideally, the only option she will think about. Eliminate the competition, and make it so you are the only one she sees."

Lex looked at Declan for a response, but Declan stared straight ahead, watching Stan pull Destiny in closer for a slower part of the song. All Declan could think about was that he never wanted to see her in the arms of another man ever again.

Chapter 10

Monday, April 23, 2011

"HEY! DECLAN, LEX!" A girl with pencil-straight blond hair wearing a short skirt and pink halter-top waved at them from down the hall as she and her darker-haired, twin-like friend made their way over. "We missed you two at the after-prom party Saturday night!"

"You mean bowling?" Declan asked. "We were there."

"No, silly," the darker haired one added as she reached up and slid his tie between her fingers, "the after, after party." Declan took a half step back and straightened his tie as the girl pouted.

Lex laughed. "Oh, that one. Sorry girls, I had a party of my own to attend, and my friend here," he said, nudging Declan and mimicking the girls' pouty faces, "had a poor little broken heart to tend to."

"Awwww…" the girls responded as they stepped to each side of Declan, one grabbing an arm while leaning her head on his shoulder and the other moving her hand in circles on his back. "We could have helped with that."

Declan sighed, gave each one of the girls a half smile, and then shot Lex an icy glare. But, before he could complete it, he noticed Destiny walking past. She glanced their direction, expressionlessly took in the entire scene, then made eye contact with him, raised an eyebrow and gave a slight nod as a silent "hello" but kept walking.

"Umm…" mindlessly escaped his mouth as he slipped his arm free and stepped away from the girls. "Thank you, ladies, see you later," he said over his shoulder as he walked off. Then he called down the hallway, "Destiny, wait up!"

Destiny paused and turned to wait for him. "Hey, what's up?" She asked as he reached her side.

"Not much, I just figured we could walk to class together since we have the same one next. How was the rest of your weekend, after prom I mean?"

"It was great! Yesterday after church my dad took me to the shooting range. Oh! Check it out!" She smiled excitedly as she swung her backpack around to pull from it what looked like a rolled-up poster, then she handed it to him. "I've got skills!" she added as Declan unrolled the paper to reveal a target sheet with bullet holes surrounding the bull's-eye and three right near the center.

Declan laughed. "Skills? You got three out of what looks to be hundreds."

"What? No!" Destiny protested as she pointed at the paper, "all those shots hit the target, just because I didn't hit the middle doesn't mean they are useless. Besides, I'd like to see you do any better." She challenged playfully.

"Hah, me? I would hit that little circle every time," Declan boasted with false bravado, "my skills with a gun are legendary."

Destiny laughed as she reached over and took the poster back from him. "I'm sure they are. Have you ever even seen a gun?"

He let out a little snort. "Seen? I have seen tons of guns. My dad has a big, incredibly old, gun cabinet he keeps locked up and on display in his bedroom. Have I seen a gun? Of course! Fired one however… ehh… no, I have never fired one."

"What? Your dad owns all those guns and he hasn't shown you how to use them? Does he go hunting?"

"Yes, he goes hunting quite often with his friends, but he has never taken me. I suppose he still thinks it is too dangerous. Most likely, though, the thought of taking me has never even crossed his mind."

"Hmmm…" Destiny pursed her lips and handed him the rolled-up poster again. "Well, you should keep this then."

"Why is that?" He asked as he reached out his hand to accept it.

"Just consider it a resumé for the future," she said with a mischievous smile. "A fragile, wealthy young man like yourself is going to need to hire a bodyguard someday. This will remind you to give me a call."

Declan laughed and shook his head. "I will hang it on my bedroom wall, so as to never forget." He lightly bopped her on the head with it.

"Good," she said with a smile. "So, how was your weekend?"

"Uneventful," he answered as he clasped his hands behind his back.

"Really?" she asked looking at him. "Nothing of interest happened at all?"

Declan just shook his head.

"Well, did you have fun at the dance at least?"

Declan paused in his walking and his eyes glazed over in thought before he answered, "Let us just say I hope people are right when they call prom a once-in-a-lifetime experience."

Destiny laughed out loud. "I'm assuming that means you had no fun at all."

Declan shrugged as he started walking again and thought to himself, *Certainly not as much fun as Stan.*

Destiny took a couple quick steps to catch up with him and added, "You might have had more fun if you had done some dancing."

Declan gave her a small smile then looked down at the floor. "Yes, perhaps."

"Why didn't you ask someone?"

He ignored the question and quickened his pace.

"Declan?" Destiny continued with a hint of exasperation in her voice as she hustled to keep up with him. "I'm serious," she said.

As they reached their classroom door she gently grabbed one of his arms, stopping him before he entered the room. Declan looked down at her hand on his arm, sighed, and turned to face her. "Serious about what?"

"I just…" She flushed lightly. "I just want to make sure you know I'm not going to look down on you if you decide you want to date someone. Just because I don't date yet doesn't mean I'll like disown you as a friend or something if you do." She paused and looked up at him with concern in her eyes and a hesitant half smile. "You know?"

Declan stared into her eyes for a couple of seconds, once again lost in her concern for him, before responding, "You do not have to worry about that."

Destiny smiled at first but then furrowed her eyebrows in confusion. "Wait, worry about what exactly?"

Declan's eyes glazed over again as he reached out and brushed a piece of Destiny's hair from her face and behind her ear. Then he simply said, "I know my options," before turning and entering their classroom.

Chapter 11

Friday, October 21, 2011

THIS IS A NIGHTMARE, Declan groaned inwardly as he sat at his desk resting his forehead in his hands and glaring at the scene in front of him.

The science teacher was currently absent because she had misplaced the keys to the cabinet that conveniently contained all her teaching materials. So, they were left to wait, unattended, while she ran out to see if she had left them in her car.

Destiny was sitting in the front row, one desk ahead and to the left of Declan, and for her third day back at school she had outdone herself. She wore a mid-thigh length, skin-tight, black skirt with a wraparound top tied just loose enough to constantly tease that it could come undone at any second. Her hair was in a fancy up-do with a few curled strands falling down here and there, and the heels of her shoes gave her four full inches more of height. At this moment, she was giggling uncontrollably at the two guys sitting on either side of her.

"For real?" she asked in between laughs. "Someone fell for that line?"

"Yes, of course," the one on her left said, leaning in close. "But it doesn't work for just anyone. You have to have my handsome looks and boyish charm to go along with it." He gave her a wink, causing her to blush and crack up even more.

The second boy laughed along as he skooted his desk right up next to hers and chimed in. "Here's a pick-up line you'll always remember."

Destiny turned toward him and smiled. "Yes?"

He gave his biggest grin as he asked, "How much does a polar bear weigh?"

"How much?" she asked as she stifled a giggle.

The boy lifted his arms in a mock stretch and slid one of his arms around the back of her chair as he said, "Enough to break the ice."

Destiny laughed so hard she covered her face with her hands out of embarrassment; Declan leaned back in his desk and crossed his arms across his chest while he watched. Slowly the one boy's arm began moving toward her shoulder. Declan attempted to glare a hole into the arm but luckily it turned out to be unnecessary because the teacher rushed in right at that moment. Destiny choked off her laughter and the boys quickly returned to their regular seating positions. Declan sighed in relief.

"Well class," the teacher said, slightly out of breath, "I can't find my keys, which is unfortunate because today is supposed to be a review day for the test tomorrow, and we don't have time to postpone the test."

This resulted in multiple groans and protests from around the room. Destiny pursed her lips in thought and glanced around the room before raising her hand. "Yes, Destiny?" the teacher sounded exasperated.

"Ummm…" she began timidly, "if you don't mind, I could try to pick the lock."

"Pick the lock? Are you serious?" The teacher asked, crossing her arms.

"Yes, I'm pretty sure I can," Destiny added. "My dad taught me… just in case."

The teacher crossed her arms and stared at her for a full two seconds but then threw them up in surrender. "Fine, might as well give it a shot."

Destiny smiled as she pulled a bobby pin from her hair and slid out of her desk before heading to the cabinet in the back of the room.

Declan turned his head away from her as she walked past, but he couldn't avoid getting a whiff of her perfume, and it made his heart clench. Once the sound of her heels clicking on the floor stopped, he turned to watch.

She slid her shoes off and dropped down to her knees in front of the cabinet in order to have a better look at the lock, then she stuck one end of the bobby pin in and started fiddling around with it. "This may take a little bit," she said, "it's been a while since I've practiced."

"Okay, class," the teacher said, "let's play some hangman while we wait." This elicited more groans from the class, but everyone turned to the front of the room anyway. Everyone except for Declan; he continued to watch Destiny.

Her head was turned slightly so he could see that she had stuck the tip of her tongue out the side of her mouth.

A little smile broke onto his face as he recalled that she did this involuntarily every time she tried to focus.

She seemed to sense him watching, because all of a sudden she turned to look at him and made eye contact before either one knew it was happening. She narrowed her eyes at him and defiantly turned back to the cabinet, continuing with clenched teeth.

And to think I almost forgot this was a nightmare, Declan thought as he turned to face the front of the room right before hearing a "clink" and the cabinet groaning open.

The teacher's jaw dropped as Destiny announced, "It's open." The teacher laughed and smiled as she thanked Destiny and admitted she didn't think she could do it.

Destiny just smiled in return as she picked up her shoes and walked silently back to her desk where she received high fives from each of her friendly male neighbors.

Then the guy on her left brought one hand to his chest as he said, "I'd give you the key to my heart, but it would appear you don't need it." She, of course, broke into laughter and Declan sighed while rolling his eyes.

Chapter 12

DESTINY SAT ON HER bed staring through the window into the backyard. Declan and his crew were working hard, trying to dig up all the weeds and flatten out the dirt to get it ready for laying sod.

Declan looked like an entirely different person in blue jeans, a white T-shirt, and gardening gloves. Practically every inch of him was smeared in dirt, and she could tell his farmer's tan was going to be ridiculous.

Tears brimmed in her eyes, and because she was alone she let them fall softly down her cheeks as she focused her gaze closer on him, trying to see the friend she used to have—but it seemed impossible. In the last week he had morphed from a close friend to a monster who had brought one of her worst nightmares to life, and now all she could see was a stranger with similar physical features. It was like the boy she had laughed with and grown up with had never really existed, and even if he had, he was dead now, and she was the only one who knew.

When was the last time I even saw him smile? … That's not fair, she scolded herself, *he would smile if you would let him.* It was true. She realized she had been torturing him since "the event". She thought it would give her some sort of satisfaction, and it did—for a little while anyway. But it didn't change anything. She still felt lost and alone. *I don't know what to do… forgive him?* Her stomach clenched *No! I can't… not yet anyway. What he did is just so… so… horrible.* She grabbed a pillow and covered her face with it. Then a softer, quieter voice in her head whispered, *At least he didn't mean to hurt you. He was trying to help; his crime is ignorance.*

Destiny sighed and looked again into the backyard. Declan was kneeling and tugging at a humongous weed that was putting up a huge fight. As it gave way the force of it caused him to fall backwards into the dirt. Destiny let out a tiny laugh as she watched his face change from frustration as he was pulling the weed, to shock as he fell—then triumph when he saw the weed and its entire root system in his hands. Then, almost instantly he went from looking at the weed to staring up at her window, and Destiny let out a little gasp as she rolled off the bed to get out of sight.

Wow, way to be awkward, she thought as she lay on the floor for a few seconds before her embarrassment was interrupted by her mom calling up to her.

"Destiny, your dad and I are home. Why don't you come downstairs so the guys can show us the blueprints they have for the yard?"

"Coming Mom," she yelled back as she stood up and walked to the mirror to make sure there was no lingering evidence of her tears.

After checking her appearance she headed down the stairs, keeping her eyes on each stair to avoid tripping. Consequently, she failed to see Johnny who was standing with his back to her at the bottom of the stairs. He was waiting his turn to wash up in the bathroom, and she ran right into him.

"Ooof," was the only sound she made as she bounced off him and fell to a seated position on the stairs.

"Oh," Johnny responded as he spun around to see if she was okay. "I'm sorry," he said as he stifled a laugh.

"What happened?" Declan interjected as he stepped out of the bathroom. "Are you okay?" he asked Destiny as he gave Johnny a look of suspicion.

Destiny blushed and ducked her head as she answered, "I'm fine. It was my fault. I wasn't looking where I was going and ran into his back. Sorry, Johnny."

"No need to apologize," Johnny said with another laugh. "Hardly felt a thing." Then both he and Declan extended a hand to help her up.

Destiny paused for a second then reached up and took Johnny's hand, ignoring Declan's, and let Johnny pull her up.

"Thank you," she said to Johnny before continuing into the kitchen.

Declan clenched his jaw as she walked away, then rubbed his hands on his pant legs in frustration, only to realize he had gotten his hands dirty again. He sighed and stepped into the bathroom to wash them for a second time.

Once everyone was in the kitchen, they gathered around the center counter as Lex rolled out an actual blueprint sheet. Destiny snorted internally as she pictured Lex slaving over the diagram. She let a little smile escape.

"As you can see," Lex started, explaining the blueprints, "we took the liberty of drawing up some ideas, but they are pretty simple. So, if you would like us to add or subtract anything from the plans, just let us know and we will." He paused and glanced up at Mr. Ackerman.

"Sounds good to me," he responded. "What do you have?"

"Okay," Lex continued, "there is a current fad in the landscaping business…" he began, but was interrupted by a chuckle from Destiny. "What?" he asked her.

"Nothing, nothing." Destiny covered her mouth with one hand and waved him on with the other. "Sorry, continue."

Lex raised one eyebrow at her as he began explaining. "The current fad is pretty simple. Basically, people want their yards to look bigger and that means more grass, fewer plants. So, we thought it might be nice to line the fence with rosebushes—the color to be chosen by the missus here—" he said with a flourish of his hand to Destiny's mom, who grinned at him, "then in the middle of the yard we would like to create a circle of some other sort of perennial flower, the type of which is also up for grabs."

"Would tulips work?" Mrs. Ackerman asked.

Lex smiled at her. "That would be perfect. Then, Declan thought it would be a good idea to plant an apple tree right smack in the middle of the circle."

"Oh," Mr. Ackerman responded, "that sounds like a great idea. We love apples!" He wrapped one arm around Destiny's shoulder and the other around his wife and pulled them in for side hugs. Then he asked, "What kind of apples?"

"Spartan," Declan interjected abruptly, then cleared his throat.

Destiny's eyes shot up and made contact with his. She flushed as he fiercely held the eye contact and explained. "I would like to plant a Spartan apple tree because Spartans are Destiny's favorite."

"Really?" her dad asked. "I had no idea those were your favorites."

Destiny almost didn't hear her dad as she studied the pleading look in Declan's eyes and answered softly, "Yes, because of the movie *300*."

Mr. Ackerman let out a big guffaw as he gave their side hug an extra little squeeze. "I suppose that's as good a reason as any."

"Do we have a plan then?" Lex asked Mr. Ackerman.

He smiled at his wife who smiled back and then reached out to shake Lex's hand as he said, "It will be the best-looking back yard we've ever had. Don't you think so, Destiny?"

"Yep, works for me," she said glancing up at him with a forced smile. "I'm gunna go do some homework now."

"Yes, of course. We will call you down when dinner is ready," he called after her as she walked into the hallway and toward the stairs.

"Destiny?"

Destiny paused a couple of steps up and turned around. Declan must have followed her out. His arms were clasped behind his back; his hair was tousled and dried dirt clung to it. For a second, because standing on the stairs brought her above eye level with him, he reminded her of a child.

"Yes?" Her voice was flat.

He pulled his arms around and crossed them in front as he looked her straight in the eyes with his usual formal fashion, shattering the childlike illusion almost instantly. "I would like to be certain you understand what I mean to say with the Spartan apple tree."

Destiny studied his face with its stone-cold demeanor; he had even managed to mask his eyes into an emotionless state. She felt her own barriers rise as well, and she narrowed her eyes at him.

"Yes, Declan, I understand entirely what this means." She paused and eyed him up and down before adding, "Like father, like son."

Declan's mouth dropped slightly, and he took a half step back as he watched her turn around and continue up the stairs for a few seconds before he forced out, "No, Destiny… I mean, please do not think that…"

Destiny paused at the top of the stairs, sighed, and turned slightly toward him without looking at him, then said quietly, "I know Declan, I know. I'm just… tired. See you tomorrow." Then she disappeared around the corner.

Once safely in her room with the door closed and locked, she lowered the window shade and collapsed onto her bed. Then she reached into her bedside-table drawer and pulled out a picture.

Time seemed to slip by as she silently stared at a photo of what now felt like two young strangers sitting on the branch of an apple tree with their arms around each other's shoulders and smiles bursting off their faces. *What have I become?* She asked silently as she drifted off to sleep on a pillow that was damp from her tears.

Chapter 13

DECLAN SMILED WHEN he saw his mother's car in the driveway. She had been in London for the past week, and with his father in New York the house seemed unbearably empty. Declan was accustomed to being at home alone, but given the recent events he couldn't stand the idea of feeling any lonelier.

"Mother?" he called out as he entered the house.

"Yes, dear," she responded from the living room. "I'm in here."

Mrs. Rayner was tall and thin with blond hair pulled back tightly into a bun, and she wore a simple but elegant form-fitting white dress. She stood to greet him with a hug as he came into the room, but stopped as she took in the sight of him caked in dirt. She put a hand on each of his shoulders, smiled, and then patted him on the cheek instead.

"I am glad you are home, Mother." Declan smiled at her.

"As am I," she responded, eyeing him up and down. She shook her head, picked up her wine glass, and took a drink. "My, my, what kind of situation have you gotten yourself into that has you walking around looking such a mess?"

Declan sighed and sat down in one of the chairs, causing his mother to cringe. "It is a very long story."

Mrs. Rayner took a seat as well and said, "Well, I am all ears. I have absolutely no other obligations until tomorrow afternoon when I have to meet a friend in San Francisco."

Declan frowned. "You leave tomorrow already?"

"Yes, dear. It's the only free time my friend has to meet with me. But that is not the topic of discussion right now. I want to know why you were rolling around in the mud."

Declan's heart sank as he realized he would be alone again tomorrow night, but he pushed those thoughts aside to answer his mother. "The guys and I are landscaping Destiny's lawn because…"

"Destiny?" Mrs. Rayner interrupted. "Who is Destiny?"

Declan furrowed his eyebrows. "Destiny has been my friend since grade school. You have met her on several different occasions… her father is a police officer…"

"Oh! Yes, yes. I remember now. I never forget a man in uniform," she said with a chuckle and a wink. "Mother," Declan said with a groan. "Really?"

She laughed some more and placed her hand over her heart. "You're right, you're right. Terribly sorry. Please continue." She waved him on with one hand and lifted her wine glass to her lips with the other.

Declan rested his forehead in his right hand for a couple seconds before saying, "It is not really that important. We just decided to help them out as a favor."

"Oh, come on." Mrs. Rayner shook her head and wagged a finger at him. "You mean to tell me that my prim and proper son has purchased his first pair of blue jeans in order to simply 'do a favor' that involves hard physical labor and calluses on his hands? There has got to be more to this story."

She eyed him for a couple minutes while she sipped her wine and Declan sighed, looked up at the ceiling, and shook his head.

All of a sudden his mother jumped to her feet and exclaimed, "Oh, my! You have a crush on this girl!" Declan flushed red as she laughed and pinched his cheek. "My little man has a crush."

"Mother, no, that is not..." he tried to cut her off, "I mean, well... she is just my, but maybe someday..."

Mrs. Rayner ignored his stammering as she made her way back to her seat and waved a hand at him. "Go on then. Tell me about this Aphrodite that has stolen my boy's heart and made him slave away in the dirt." Declan leaned forward and looked at the floor. "Destiny is... well... she has always been there for me. She is simply just... just beautiful in every way..." He was at a loss for words and stopped speaking. He shook his head and angled his chair more directly toward his mother.

"I'm sure she is. So, then why does she have you acting like a servant?"

"It's not like that," he replied defensively. "This is my choice because it gives me a reason to be near her… to protect her."

His mother eyed him suspiciously. "Protect her? From what exactly are you protecting her?"

In the line of duty her father shot and killed a man who ended up being a member of one of the local gangs. Now the gang wants revenge and has threatened to kill Destiny."

"What?" She was shocked, and she slowly set her glass on the side table before continuing, "A gang is after this girl, and you are trying to protect her? Is that not what her father is for? He is a police officer for crying out loud!" She fanned her face with her hand. "Does *your* father know about this?"

"Yes, he does," Declan said straightforwardly, "and he has supported my decision because she is part of our… well…" He paused, and his mother shook her head. "…Mr. Ackerman cannot be with her all the time, and I can be with her when he is not. I intend to do everything within my ability to keep her safe."

Mrs. Rayner dropped her head backwards onto the couch, covered her face with her hands, and peered out through her fingers for a little bit, then lowered her hands and said, "Well, then. I already know not to counter your father. My opinion means nothing to him, and I learned a long time ago not to waste the energy. Just promise me you will do your best to stay safe."

Declan frowned. "I will try to stay safe, but mother you should know, I think father does care about you."

"Ha! I am sorry dear, but it has been many, many years since he gave me any reason to believe that to be true."

"What makes you say that? I mean, what sort of things would he have to do to make you see he cares?"

She smiled wryly and picked up her glass. "To start with, he could take the time to listen to me and at least try to understand my point of view on things, but he does not." She chuckled a little as she took a drink and said, "Actually, I do not remember a time when he did." Then she looked at Declan sternly. "This girl, Destiny, you say you care for her. Let me give you some advice since you seem willing to throw yourself in harm's way for her. Make certain she knows you care."

"I do. I mean, I have… I think. I mean, I have made sure she is under twenty-four-hour surveillance so that she will not be harmed."

His mother furrowed her eyebrows. "That is not at all what I mean. I am referring to using words—talking to her. You need to tell her how you feel, straightforward and simple. Then you need to live it out."

"Okay… but *how* do I live it out?"

"There are many ways. You can start by respecting her for who she is. Honor her desires, whatever they may be, even if you do not understand them."

Declan felt his face turning red; he lowered his eyes to the floor and clasped his hands in his lap.

Mrs. Rayner stood up, put a finger under his chin, and lifted his face, forcing him to look at her. "Listen, I know your father and I are a poor example of a healthy relationship, and I am sorry for that. But, that gives you all the more reason to be smart and deliberate about your actions with this girl. Chances are your natural instincts are going to be wrong."

Declan's eyes watered a little as he looked up at his mother. He had never had such an honest conversation with her before, and he longed for more. "I may have already messed up," he choked out.

She moved her finger from his chin and turned toward the kitchen. "Well then, apologize," she said. "If she is as important to you as you are letting on, then do not let a ridiculous thing like your pride get in the way. I need to refill my glass and then I am off to bed." She turned and pointed at him. "You, young man, need to take a shower. I will see you in the morning for breakfast before I leave."

Declan started to let her walk away, then he stood and blurted out, "Mother."

"Yes, Declan?" she called from the kitchen.

"I love you."

There was silence for a couple of seconds, then she called back softly, "I love you too, dear."

Chapter 14

Sunday, October 23, 2011

DESTINY STARED OUT the car window as she listened to her parents chatter back and forth about the sermon. It had been a beautiful lesson about marriage, and it had made Destiny feel horrible. Her parents had tried to console her and tell her once again she wasn't to blame for what had happened to her, but she just smiled and shrugged them off. All she wanted was to get home where she could have some time alone with her thoughts. But, as they pulled onto their street she realized that was going to be next to impossible.

"Oh yeah," Mr. Ackerman said as he spotted Declan's red Lexus, "I forgot I told the guys they could come over today to get some work done on the yard."

"Good thing I have plenty for lunch," her mom chimed in. "We should insist they eat with us."

As they pulled into the driveway Declan came around the corner of the house, his face smeared in dirt and a shovel over his shoulder. When he spotted them he smiled, waved, and headed toward them.

"How was church?" he asked no one in particular as they got out of the car.

"The sermon was from First Corinthians," Mr. Ackerman answered as he reached out and patted Declan on the back. "The pastor laid it out very well."

"You should join us next time," Mrs. Ackerman said as she lifted her purse strap over her shoulder.

Declan smiled and looked at Destiny, who was already heading to the front door. "Maybe I will, if it is okay with Destiny."

Destiny paused and glanced over her shoulder. "Yeah, you should come," she said dryly as she stepped inside.

The three of them stood there for a second, their smiles fading slowly, before Declan asked, "Is she okay?"

"Yeah, yeah," her dad reassured him. "She's probably just tired is all; she needs some rest."

Mrs. Ackerman pulled out a big smile and changed the subject. "We're having hamburgers for lunch. Tell your friends to wash up, because you're all expected to join us."

Declan nodded cordially and smiled. "Thank you, ma'am. I'll go tell them now."

The guys were all happy to take a break from their work as they piled into the house and rushed to the bathroom to clean up. Declan trailed behind them, laughing lightly as he watched them push each other around trying to be first, but he got distracted as he walked past the staircase and noticed Destiny standing near the top of the stairs staring at something. He made his way up toward her to see what was going on.

As he reached her, he noticed that she seemed to be lost in her own little world, her eyes glossed over as she stared at an old photograph that was setting on a tiny decorative table in the hallway. A couple beamed out from the picture, full of excitement on their wedding day.

"Hey, is something wrong?" He asked softly.

Destiny jumped then turned slightly in his direction as her eyes re-focused. "Oh, no. Nothing's wrong." She shook her head, but it was obvious that wasn't true, so he just stood there waiting. Destiny swallowed and blinked away a layer of liquid that had formed over her eyes as she turned back toward the photo. "It's just a picture of my parents on their wedding day."

Declan looked at the photo. "They look happy," he said, and then paused before adding, "so, why are you upset?"

A short, ironic-sounding laugh escaped Destiny's lips as she responded coldly, "You don't really want me to answer that question."

"I would not have asked you if I did not care to know the answer," he stated earnestly. "What is bothering you, Destiny?"

She glanced up at him, and the concern on his face caught her off-guard. "Okay, then," she started with a sigh, "I was just thinking about the dress."

"The wedding dress?" Declan asked, puzzled.

"Yes," she continued. "Growing up, I always wanted a marriage like the one my parents have. They are happy, they love each other unconditionally, and they know that neither one will ever leave the other."

"Yeah, I have always wondered how they pulled that off."

Destiny lowered her eyes from his and turned back to the photo as she clasped her hands nervously behind her back. "They pull it off because they follow God's instructions for marriage. It makes sense." She motioned with one hand, raising it palm-side-up into the air. "God invented marriage, so it's wise to follow His instructions on how to make it work."

Declan kept watching her face as she stared at the picture. "I can see that, but what does it have to do with the dress?"

"It shows off how they started their marriage. Wedding dresses are white because they symbolize purity…" Destiny choked up a little on that last word and covered her mouth to cough a couple times before continuing. "They were both virgins when they got married, and they have been with no one else sexually. No one in their past to compare each other to, no questions of loyalty, complete trust—knowing that they have trusted each other with their most precious possession and have been trusted equally in return." Tears began to flow freely from her eyes. "I… I no longer deserve… I no longer deserve a white dress."

Declan jumped to her defense, "That is not true. You are the purest person I know. You have nothing to be ashamed of."

"No, Declan, my virginity is gone," she said between slightly clenched teeth as she tried to bring her tears under control and wipe them from her face with her hands.

"That should not matter." Declan moved closer, his arms reaching out to her, but she stepped out of his reach so he just continued talking. "You are the kindest, most considerate person I know. I have always admired you for that. This is not a big deal; it was necessary. You have got to stop blaming yourself."

Her tears dried as she bristled in irritation. "It does matter, Declan." She wiped her face dry and crossed her arms, looking him straight in the eyes. Her voice was low and she spoke with a bit of malice. "It is a big deal. The fact is, Declan, you… you raped me." She pointed firmly at him and then back at herself for emphasis. "And it can never be taken back." The tears began flowing again. "I can never be pure, ever again." She lowered her head, crossing one arm over her stomach and covering her eyes with her other hand as she struggled to not sob and failed.

Stunned, Declan's jaw dropped. He had never seen her this distraught, and he hated it. His stomach churned. This was all his fault. He had to do something or say something to make her feel better. So, he stepped closer to her and put his left hand on her shoulder.

"Destiny, please look at me," he said softly but firmly.

Destiny shook her head but then gave in and turned to him, looking up to meet his gaze.

"This is entirely my fault," he said with water brimming in his eyes. "Not yours. You did nothing wrong." He put his right hand on his chest still keeping his left hand on her shoulder. "I made this decision because I could not stand the thought of anyone hurting you." Then he reached out and brushed her hair from her face, but the moment he did he realized the mistake he had made as her face turned instantly pale. Seconds later she was grabbing her stomach, bending over at the waist, and throwing up all over the carpet.

Destiny dropped to her knees, shocked at the emotions raging through her system. Her mind was consumed with images and feelings of desperation and hopelessness from that night. Images and emotions she had been trying to ignore and move on from, but now they had broken free and she had lost control.

Declan's eyes widened as he watched her keel over in pain. *What is going on? What happened? What did I do?* Endless amounts of frantic questions rushed through his mind as he dropped to his knees beside her and reached out to try and help by holding her hair back while she threw up.

"No! No!" Destiny insisted as she waved her hand in his face and motioned for him to step back. "Don't touch me!"

"What?" he said sheepishly, "I just want to help." He placed his hands on each of her shoulders again.

This time she gasped, turned toward him and shoved him away, causing herself to fall backwards as she yelled out at the top of her lungs, "Dad! Mom! DAD! HELP!"

Declan also fell backwards from her shove, surprised at the strength of it, and ended up sitting with his back against a wall as he watched her call for her parents. He was stunned and unsure of what he should do. He didn't want to watch her suffer, so as she threw up again he moved to help, but hesitated and froze as he realized: *If I touch her, I just make things worse. I can't... I can't even touch her.* At that moment all hope of redemption drained out of him as he watched the person he cared most about in the world suffer by just a touch of his hand. *What have I done?*

"Destiny! What's the matter? What's going on?" Mrs. Ackerman was frantic as she ran up the stairs, but it was Destiny's dad who got to her first.

He knelt down next to her, placing one hand on her back as he looked over at Declan and asked, "What happened?"

Declan just stared at them, his jaw slightly drooping; face pale and eyes wide.

Then her mom arrived at her side, wrapped her arms around her waist, and pulled her to a standing position. "Come on, honey, let's get you to the bathroom to clean up," she said gently as she led her down the hallway.

Mr. Ackerman stayed behind and watched them go, then turned to Declan, who was now staring at a blank wall with the same expression on his face.

"Declan," he said as he took a sitting position next to the boy. "Can you tell me what happened?"

Declan seemed to hear him for the first time and responded slightly above a whisper, "I'm not sure. I just wanted to make her feel better. I barely touched her."

"She started throwing up because you touched her?"

"Her hair."

"You touched her hair?"

Declan nodded slightly. "She was crying, her hair was in her eyes, I thought… get it out of the way."

"I see." Mr. Ackerman sighed as he pulled one knee up and stretched the other leg out. "You may have triggered a memory key."

"A what?" Declan seemed to barely be paying attention, but Destiny's dad continued anyway.

"Doctors warned us of it. When she was drugged that night it wiped out a lot of her memory about what happened, but they said that with time some memories might return and that certain things may speed up that process, causing tidal waves of memories and emotions to break through." He cracked his knuckles. "So, no reason for you to be feeling so badly about this. It was not your fault. In fact, it may be for the best it happened now, because it means she is a tiny bit closer to allowing herself to heal."

Declan had regained his composure but was still a little sheepish when he said, "I just do not understand how this is affecting her so much."

Mr. Ackerman seemed confused. "What do mean?"

"I mean…" Declan hesitated but decided to continue, "what happened to her that night was unfortunate, but she is alive and healthy now. She should be able to move on, right? It was only physical and she is physically healthy, so why is she so emotional about it?"

Mr. Ackerman laughed awkwardly then cleared his throat before responding in a serious but understanding tone. "Well, I think the fact that she is emotional about it proves it is not just physical. The reality is, sex is never just physical, and trying to pretend it is goes against our very nature and robs us of enjoying life the way we were designed to."

Declan looked down at his hands and watched as his fingers rubbed the fabric on the leg of his jeans. Mr. Ackerman paused to watch Declan's fingers as well before saying, "That's funny; Destiny has a similar nervous tic."

Startled, Declan pulled his hands away. "I am sorry; I have never done that before. I do not know why…"

"Not really the type to have emotional tells, are you?" he stated as he placed a hand on Declan's shoulder. "Emotions are nothing to be ashamed of; we all have them. The key is not letting them rule your decisions, because, the majority of the time, they will lead you down the wrong path. Typically, a selfish one," he added with a little chuckle.

Declan looked at the man and asked, "Do you think Destiny will ever be the same again?"

Mr. Ackerman sighed. "Unfortunately, no one is ever the same after something traumatic happens to them. It just so happens that what Destiny went through is one of the most traumatic things a person can go through."

"She wanted to be a virgin on her wedding day," Declan said quietly as he crossed his arms and looked down again. Then he seemed to gain determination and looked back up at the wall in front of him before continuing, "But, it seems highly unlikely she would have been anyway, hardly anybody is. I just do not see why it is such a big deal."

Mr. Ackerman creased his brow as he spoke sternly but softly. "It is not as impossible as you may think, nor is it unreasonable to expect. Marriage is a commitment to being monogamous, and the foolish thing is that people think they can have sex with whoever they want before marriage but then just stop and be committed to one person after they get married. Self-control and faithfulness are habits that need to be formed, not just individual choices."

"Okay, what about practice though? It is important to be good at sex otherwise your wife might eventually turn to somebody else."

This time Mr. Ackerman let out a deep guffaw. "If neither of you have slept with anyone else, you would have no one else to compare it to. How would either of you know if someone else could be better at it? Plus, half the fun is having someone you are so intimate with that you can enjoy learning about it together with no fear of judgment from the other. Besides, the majority of problems in marriages are because of the couple comparing each other to past flings. It causes insecurity and distrust. Saving sex until after you are married eliminates a ton of baggage that could weigh you both down. Knowing you are the only one who has ever been given the gift of intimacy with that person promotes security and trust—two very important things for a healthy union."

Declan just sat there soaking it all in. He did have to admit that the idea of a woman saving herself for him really did seem appealing. No man wants to see or even contemplate the idea of his girl with some other man, so to know she had never been with another man would be priceless.

"Don't get me wrong though," Mr. Ackerman added almost getting lost in his own thoughts, "mutual sexual purity between couples does not guarantee a perfect marriage. Marriage is a lot of work, especially on certain days when the emotions seem to have run dry. Of course, in the long run all the work in the world would be worth it to know you will always have someone who cares about you by your side throughout life. There are definitely many things that factor into a marriage; sexual purity is just one of them that would make it all a whole lot easier."

"Destiny understands all of this," Declan stated, more for himself.

"Yes, she does," Mr. Ackerman said, "and she understands what she lost, which is why this is incredibly hard for her."

"She just always seems so in control. Until today, I thought she had moved on already."

"Well son." He patted Declan's shoulder again. "That's because despite her emotional tells, like fiddling with things with her fingers or tapping her foot, she likes to keep her problems to herself. She has never really enjoyed burdening other people with them, no matter how much we wish she would allow us to take some of the weight for her."

"I should have known." Declan shook his head. "I had no idea how much this event would—did affect her. But I should have seen it in her eyes, the pain. I just did not want to admit it because it is like admitting things will never be the same again."

"You know though, just because things won't be the same doesn't mean they will always be bad," her dad said sincerely. "My daughter is a strong girl who judges reality based on facts and truths, not emotions. The facts are, she was a victim in this situation and should not feel guilty, but even if she cannot accept that, or even if she were guilty, she knows God loves her unconditionally, and so do I, and so does her mom. I do believe all she needs is time to allow the emotions to drain so that she can take control again and be willing to receive love, even if she thinks she doesn't deserve it."

They sat in silence; Declan feeling closer to understanding Destiny—the girl he had admired since childhood—than he had ever felt before, and Mr. Ackerman saying a silent prayer for his daughter. Unfortunately, after a few moments, their reverie was abruptly interrupted by Mr. Ackerman's work pager. As he checked it, Mrs. Ackerman rushed out of the bathroom with an urgent look on her face.

Chapter 15

"THERE HAS BEEN A BOMB threat to one of the subway stations downtown," Mrs. Ackerman explained as she pulled on a jacket, opened the front door, then turned to Destiny. "I'm sorry honey, I have to go. We will talk more when I get back, okay?"

Destiny stood at the bottom of the staircase, leaning against the railing, her face still pale as she watched her mom rush around. The hospital had called while her mom was helping her clean up, and they needed all available EMTs to report in just in case an attack really did happen.

"Yeah, don't worry, Mom. I'll be fine," Destiny assured her.

"Yes sir, I am on my way now," Mr. Ackerman spoke into his cell phone as he hustled down the stairs with Declan close behind. "I am being called to the subway as well. I'll see you there, honey," he said to his wife as she nodded and closed the door behind her. He paused in front of his daughter and just stood there for a moment, conflicted.

"I will be okay, Dad. I'll set the security alarm; you can go," Destiny said calmly.

"I don't know. I would rather you not be alone—or even here at all. Most of the police force will be across town at the subway. Even if the alarm goes off, we might not get to you in time…"

Declan stepped to his side. "What if I take her to my house, sir? If the gang decided to attack now they would come here, but they might not think of checking my place."

"Good idea. Get her away from here." Mr. Ackerman grabbed his car keys and held his hand out to shake Declan's.

Destiny started to protest but decided against it and instead made an obvious effort to avoid eye contact with Declan.

"Destiny," her father asked, "are you okay with that?"

She paused a second, swallowed, then said, "Yeah, I'll do whatever you think is best."

"Good," he said, relieved, and pulled her into a hug. "I love you. I'll come find you as soon as I'm free." Then he was out the door.

Declan stepped toward her. "Destiny, I…"

She interrupted him, "Not now. Let's just do what needs to be done."

Declan hesitated, then pulled out his cell phone, hitting the first number on speed dial. "Lex?"

"Yeah, it's me." Lex answered his phone coolly.

"Where are you?"

"The boys and I went for a walk." He explained. "When we heard Destiny call for her parents we decided it would be courteous to give them some space."

Declan sighed. "How long will it take you to get back?"

"I don't know; maybe half an hour. It seemed a long walk would be necessary."

"That is too long. I cannot wait for you."

Lex fell silent for a second as he caught on that something was wrong. "What do you mean? What's going on, Declan?"

"There has been a bomb threat at the subway. Both of Destiny's parents have been called down there. I have to take her to my place in case it's a diversion." He looked at Destiny who was still leaning against the railing and now gazing aimlessly at the ceiling. "Call your driver and have him pick you guys up. Get to my house as soon as you can."

"Got it."

Declan grabbed Destiny's jacket and tossed it to her. "Let's go."

Destiny silently put the jacket on and followed him out the door to his car.

Once in the car, Destiny took to staring out the window with her arms crossed as Declan drove, glancing over at her every few seconds.

"I have something I need to tell you," he said after working up the courage. Destiny just kept staring out the window. "I should have said it a long time ago. I mean, I tried to say it, but I never used words; I should have used words." He looked over at her again but got no response. "What I mean to say is, I am sorry." He took a deep breath. "I am sorry for what I did to you. I should have listened to what you said and respected your decision, but I was selfish."

Destiny caught her breath as she tried to fight back tears. Declan noticed and rushed on.

"I did not understand why you would risk your life for it, but after talking to your dad, I think I do now. Or, at least, I understand your view on it better—enough to realize I hurt you…" This time it was Declan catching his breath. "You are the one person I never wanted to hurt, and yet I did… I may have even hurt you in the worst way possible and… and I am sorry. Sorrier than you could possibly know…" He stopped as he saw a single tear run down Destiny's cheek, and he quickly looked away, suddenly at a loss for words.

Just then the car jerked forward from an impact to their rear bumper.

"What the…?" He checked his rearview mirror. Adrenaline filled his body, and he slammed his foot on the gas.

Destiny placed one hand on the dashboard to steady herself as she quickly turned to look through the back window. Instead of fear hitting her as she had imagined it would when she again saw those ridiculous plastic monkey faces; the sight only invoked anger. Those jerks had caused her and her family too much trouble. Seeing them in the flesh was a reminder that they were only human; she almost felt liberated by being in their presence again.

"Call your father," Declan commanded as he tossed her his phone while quickly weaving in and out of traffic.

Destiny did just as he said.

"Dad?" she asked, almost too calmly.

"Yes, Destiny, is everything okay?" Mr. Ackerman sounded worried and stressed.

"Not exactly," she said as she looked through the rear window again and saw that the car carrying the five gang members was doing a pretty good job of tailing Declan. "We are being followed by the monkey-masked men." She chuckled a little, which caused Declan to shoot her a confused glance. "Monkey masks are so ridiculous," she added pointlessly.

"I was worried that might happen," Mr. Ackerman stated seriously, ignoring her out-of-sorts attitude. "The bomb squad found the alleged bomb right away and it turns out it was a fake. Probably a decoy to leave you unprotected. Tell Declan to try to lose them, but continue to his house. We are on our way there. If you get there before us, have him drive around the neighborhood in circles until we arrive."

"What is he saying?" Declan asked.

"Bomb was a decoy, try to lose them, keep going to your house, cops will meet us there, keep driving around the block until they get there," she rattled the information off as one would a grocery list.

Declan's face paled as he looked down at his gages, "That will be a problem. My car is pretty much on empty. We barely have enough to make it to my house. I was planning on filling up on the way home tonight."

"We are going to run out of gas," Destiny relayed blandly to her dad.

Mr. Ackerman thought silently for a couple of seconds and then said urgently, "Then you two need to find somewhere to hide until we can get to you. His house will be the best bet since Declan knows his way around and the gang does not. Do you understand?"

"Yes, Dad, I understand."

"Good. Destiny, I will get there as fast as possible. I love you."

"I love you too, Dad." Destiny choked out and cleared her throat as she hung up and explained to Declan. "We need to hide out in your house."

Declan nodded, and after a few seconds he said, "Destiny…" but was interrupted.

"No, Declan, I am not okay," she said sternly. "Don't even bother asking."

He sighed. "I know… I was not going to… I just think we should make a plan for when we get to my house. My parents are both out of town, so the house will be empty and we will definitely beat the police there. The master bedroom is the best bet for hiding. My parents have a bolt lock on the inside of their walk-in closet door, sort of like a safe room. Do you remember how to get there?"

"Yes," she said, then added, sounding annoyed, "but couldn't I just follow you anyway?"

"I will not be with you," he explained. "I am going to lead them away from you to buy you more time."

For the first time since she got in the car, Destiny turned to look at him. "They will most likely kill you if they catch you."

"I know." He swallowed. This time it was Declan avoiding *her* gaze. He chuckled. "Besides, after what I did to you, I need to do something to tip the scales in my favor if I hope to make it into Heaven. Maybe sacrificing myself to save your life will be enough."

Destiny snorted in annoyance and crossed her arms again. "You have never really listened to anything I've ever said, have you?" She looked at him accusingly.

Declan looked confused but was stopped mid-thought as he realized they were coming up to his house, and he urgently changed the subject.

"Okay, so I will pull into the garage. You jump out right away and run inside and to my parent's closet, then lock yourself in and wait quietly. I will lead them upstairs, as far away from you as I possibly can. Got it?"

Destiny nodded. Declan turned toward her as much as he could behind the wheel and gave her a look that made her think he was going to explode with emotion. She quickly turned away, embarrassed.

As they pulled into the garage, Declan suddenly reached over, took her hand in his, and said, "One more thing, in case I never see you again." Destiny almost yanked her hand away but stopped when she saw the urgency in his face. "I know you hate me now, and I deserve it. But I need you to know... I knew it from the first time I saw you, but now I need to make sure I say it... I love you. Destiny, I love you," he said the second time almost as a whisper but with strong emotional force behind it.

Destiny let out a tiny gasp as she caught her breath, then looked him straight in the eye for a quick second before lowering her eyes and replying softly, "I know." She removed her hand from his and stepped out of the car.

Declan watched her make her way to the door of the house then jumped out of the car himself and rushed after her. They crossed through the kitchen and into the main entryway by the base of the staircase. Destiny stopped suddenly and turned to give Declan one last look. They stood there staring at each other and catching their breath for a few seconds until they heard glass shatter from one of the living room windows followed by the clamor of people climbing through it.

"Go!" Declan urged quietly but firmly.

Destiny obeyed, stepping around the corner into the hallway and running full-sprint toward the master bedroom.

Declan watched her disappear, and started up the stairs, pausing at the top to make sure the guys pursuing them saw him there.

"This way!" one of them yelled, "they're upstairs!"

Once he was certain they were coming, Declan ducked into the nearest bedroom. He ran across the room to the closet where he loudly opened and closed the door, then placed himself firmly in front of it as if to guard it, and awaited his fate.

Meanwhile, Destiny stumbled into the master bedroom. *What a jerk!* She screamed inwardly. *A scale to get into heaven! Why didn't he ever listen to me?* Tears streamed down her face, and in her distracted mind-set, she tripped over a briefcase, fell to the ground, and rolled sideways, coming to a stop next to a large wooden display case. Destiny gazed at it for a second before realizing what it was, but once she did, determination consumed her as she noticed it had a simple key lock.

She reached up to her hair and pulled out a bobby pin.

Chapter 16

DECLAN STRUGGLED TO SLOW his breathing. Half the battle would be appearing calm. He had to stall them as long as he could.

"I heard something in the first room to the left," he heard one of the masked men say.

"Good job, boys," another, perhaps their leader, congratulated them. "They've got nowhere else to go now."

Declan stared at the door, waiting for them to appear. Seconds seemed like hours, and he decided he might as well try to do something useful with his time, so he shot up a prayer. *Hello God, I know you have no reason to listen to me, because I never really pay you any attention, but Destiny does. She is one of the good ones, one of yours, and I just want to ask you for help to get her out of this mess.* At that moment, the first of the men appeared in the doorway. Declan took a deep breath then finished up, *Thank you, ummm... Amen.*

"Well, well, what do we have here?" The man inquired while the other four filed in behind him.

Declan crossed his arms as he stated calmly, "You are trespassing. Leave now, and I will not press any charges."

This invoked all sorts of laughter from the plastic monkey faces as the leader spoke again. "I've got a better idea. You give us the girl without a struggle, and we let you live another day to enjoy your big fancy house."

"What do you want with her?" Declan asked, keeping his face blank and taking a half step toward the closet as if to block it off.

"Please." The leader guffawed and placed one hand on his chest. "I thought we had already made that clear; a life for a life and all that jazz." He lowered his voice to a more sinister level and added, "Her father killed one of ours, so we kill one of his. Nothing personal to her, really. In fact, I wish she had a brother or something. Then we could kill him and I could just take her for myself." He paused and tapped his fake-monkey chin, watching Declan tense at his last words. "Oh, it would seem I am not the only one who noticed her beauty, am I? Tell me, what is it like to have someone like that all to yourself?"

Declan tightened his jaw while his eyes scanned the guys, watching as they fanned out to create a half-circle around him.

"What?" the man continued, "does she not belong to you?"

Declan locked his eyes on the man's as he responded with an even tone, "She is not a possession."

"Hah!" the man released, wrapping his arms around his waist while slightly bending over. "Think what you want, but as far as I'm concerned, she is all mine now. Don't worry though, maybe I won't kill her right away. I think we will have a little fun first. You can rest easy knowing that I will give her the time of her life before I end it. After all, it is the least I can do." He raised his arms into a little shrug.

Declan's blood boiled. He clenched his fists as he growled, "You will never touch her!"

The monkey man crossed his arms. "Hmmm, I do like a challenge. Let's get started then. I don't have all day." He waved both his arms to motion his cronies into action.

Declan raised his fists to his chin and crouched into a boxing position. "Do you always get others to do your dirty work for you?"

The man sighed. "Oh, please. Let's all be honest here. There is no way you are winning this fight, so why should I bother with the messy stuff? I might as well just enjoy the show."

A half-smile, half-grimace rose to Declan's face. He didn't have to win. All he had to do was stall for time. It could not be much longer now, only a few minutes.

The man on his far right was the first to throw a punch. Declan ducked it and came up strong with an uppercut to his jaw, sending the man sprawling backwards, but his success was short-lived when one of the other men stepped up from behind and swept his feet out from under him.

Declan fell sideways hard, hitting his right shoulder against the closet door.

"Ooooo…" The leader pulled his shoulders in and clasped his hands together in a mock cringe then cupped his hands around his mouth to yell at the closet door, "Hear that, girly? That's your knight in shining armor getting knocked off his high horse. Don't you worry though; we will show you what real men are like."

Declan glared at the man, but before he could get to his feet another monkey kicked him right in the middle of his back, causing him to drop to his hands and knees, allowing the fourth monkey to kick into his gut. Declan fell to his side, clasping his stomach and gasping for air as two of the monkeys continued to kick any spot he left unguarded. Finally, the leader raised his hands in a "stop" motion.

"Okay, okay, fine job boys, but that's enough. I want him conscious to watch us take his girly from him. Just pull him out of the way of that closet door."

The four goons moved to grab Declan, who tried to kick them away as best he could, but there were just too many of them, and they each grabbed one of his limbs and pulled him into the center of the room as their leader guffawed at his petty efforts to get free.

"Any final requests before we make this defeat official?" the leader asked Declan as he placed his hand on the door knob of the closet.

"Please... please," Declan gasped still struggling with his lungs. "She does not deserve this... she is the nicest person I know, would never hurt anyone..." His own lungs interrupted his plea by forcing out loud, raspy coughs, spattering blood around, but once it stopped, he continued. "Take me instead... please, do not even open that door."

"Eww!" the monkey leader responded. "You expect me to watch that nasty display of germ-spreading and actually fulfill your request? Disgusting!" He shook his head and sighed. "Well, time to get this over with," he said as he opened the door. "Come out, come out, wherever you are."

Declan watched the back of the man's head as he stared into the empty closet. Silence filled the room, and the sound of sirens in the distance began to get louder and louder as a wry smile grew on Declan's face.

In an instant, the leader spun around and yelled, "Where is she! No more games! TELL ME NOW!"

Declan grinned at him with a blood-filled smile and said quietly, "Like I said, you will never touch her."

"I will have you killed this instant if you don't tell me where she is!" the leader threatened as the sirens wailed loudly and came to a stop right outside the house.

"Better do it fast. You are running out of time," Declan answered coolly.

The leader growled and kicked Declan right in the gut, took a couple of deep breaths, and gave the order, "Do it! Kill him now!"

With that last kick Declan's world began to fade around him. He lay flat on his back staring up at the ceiling as the gang members looked down on him. He could vaguely make out a knife in one of the man's hands, but he didn't care. He had held them off until the cops arrived. Sure, they wouldn't be able to save him, but Destiny would be safe. He closed his eyes and told himself it would be okay to drift off to sleep. But, just before the darkness engulfed him a sharp explosion ricocheted throughout the room, followed by frantic yelling. Intrigued, he tried to open his eyes, but his eyelids fought him as if they were made of lead. All he could do was think, *was that a gunshot?* Then nothing.

Chapter 17

MEMORIES FLOATED THROUGH Declan's mind as time seemed to no longer exist.

Standing side-by-side with Lex in long robes as they took their oaths of membership to their secret society… his mother's voice as she told him she loved him… a single golden apple flying through the air and hitting Jesse in the shoulder… his father straightening his tie… Mr. Ackerman with one arm around his wife and the other arm around his daughter…

The memories grew darker as he watched his own parents fighting while he hid behind the railing high up on the stairs. Tears were streaming down his mother's face as she grabbed whatever was within reach and hurled it at his father who was stomping around, red in the face, and bellowing at the top of his lungs. He saw his father grab his car keys and slam the door on his way out. Then his mother threw one last vase at the closed door before falling onto the couch and weeping uncontrollably. Tears fell down Declan's cheeks as he watched, but the memory was interrupted by the sound of girlish laughter that seemed to come from an entirely different world, and he turned toward it.

It was Destiny, her dark hair glowing, her smile radiating light, and her eyes sparkling with joy as she extended her hand toward him. Declan felt hope fill his body, and he reached out his hand, but just before he was able to grab hold of hers a voice in the distance interrupted, "Come on man, you've got to wake up now." Declan turned his head back and forth trying to find the source of it as it continued, "Wake up, dude."

"Lex?" Declan questioned, "where are…"

Suddenly it felt like a giant vacuum appeared out of nowhere and sucked Declan backward through a tunnel of light. Then everything stopped abruptly, and the world went dark.

"Just open your eyes, man," he heard Lex plead.

Open my…? he thought, and slowly light began draining through his eyelids as they opened wider and wider.

"Dude!" Lex yelled. "You're awake!"

Declan looked around the room. Everything seemed white except for Lex, who was sitting right next to his bed in a disheveled black suit.

"Where am I?" Declan's voice came out raspy and thin.

"The hospital, man," Lex answered. "You've been out all night—it's Monday afternoon. The doctors thought you would be in a coma for a while, but I didn't like that idea, so I've been here trying to wake you up." A grin broke out on Lex's face. "It would appear to have worked."

"A coma?" Declan whispered as his eyes wandered the room. Then in an instant the confusion turned to fear. "Destiny!" he called out while sitting up suddenly, but pain shot through his body and he fell right back down. "Ugghh…" he groaned.

Lex stood up next to the bed, raising his hands in a stop motion. "Whoa, dude! Don't move! Geez!" He shook his head. "You've got like five hundred broken bones or something. You're lucky to be alive."

"Five hundred?" Declan asked.

"Well, more like three ribs, one forearm, and a crack in your right shin. But the internal bleeding was ridiculous. They said you would have bled to death if the ambulance had taken even six more minutes."

Declan shook his head. "I do not care about that. How is Destiny?"

Lex gave him a crooked smile and sat back down in his chair, slouching back and crossing his arms. "Declan, Declan, always singing the same old tune." He laughed, then added, "Destiny is perfectly fine and safe at home. You don't have to worry about her anymore."

Declan slowly exhaled with relief and closed his eyes.

"Actually," Lex continued with a laugh, "it would seem you really didn't have to worry about her to begin with. It's all kind of ironic."

Declan opened his eyes and looked at Lex. "What do you mean?"

Lex sat up straight, gripping the armrests as he explained, "She saved your life, man."

"What?" Confusion flooded through Declan as he tried to remember the events of the night before.

"I know, dude, it's crazy stuff. Here we all were thinking she hated you and whatnot, but then there she goes saving your life."

Declan shot Lex a glare. "No, I mean, how did she save my life?"

"Oh." Lex stood up and leaned against one of the railings on Declan's bed. "Well, apparently just as those evil jerks where going to slice your throat open, Destiny barged into the room and shot the leg of the one who was holding the knife to your throat. Then she turned the gun on the leader, threatened him into backing them all up against the wall, and made them wait there until the cops rushed in a few minutes later. The guys and I arrived shortly after that, missed all the excitement." He feigned irritation but then got serious again. "They would have bled you dead if she hadn't shown up, dude."

Declan's mouth fell open as he stared at the wall behind Lex. "She was supposed to be hiding," he said more to himself. "Where did she get the…"

Lex interrupted his thoughts, "She says she picked the lock on your father's gun cabinet. Pretty impressive if you ask me." He chuckled as he rubbed his fingernails against the front of his jacket and then glanced down at them as if checking for smudges.

Declan kept staring at the wall in shock for a few seconds, but then the door burst open and his mother rushed in.

Strands of her hair where flying about, loose from her normally tight bun, as she rushed to Declan's bed and leaned over him kissing him on the cheek and saying, "Oh, my dear! I hopped on a plane as soon as I heard. I was so frightened!"

Declan smiled weakly. "I am okay, Mother. Really."

Mrs. Rayner placed a hand on each side of his face and made pouty lips at him, then she reached over and took Lex's hand in hers. "Thank you for looking after him this whole time."

Lex smiled and nodded. "It wasn't a problem."

She smiled back at him and then turned her attention to Declan. "Your father is on his way also. He should be here by tonight." She reached into her purse and pulled out her phone as she stood up. "Actually, if you would temporarily excuse me, I need to call him and inform him that you are awake." She reached down and patted Declan lightly on the cheek before turning and leaving the room.

Declan watched her leave and then turned back to Lex. "So, the gang, where are they? Is Destiny really safe now?"

"Yes, it's over," Lex reassured him, and then went on to explain. "The police arrested the guys who were at your house right away, and one of those cowards actually rolled over on the rest of the gang within the first hour of questioning. He gave up all their names and enough evidence to have each one of them thrown into jail for the rest of their lives. The cops have been rounding them up all night." He reached down and tapped Declan on the nose with his index finger and added in a cutesy voice, "You and your little princess charming have nothing more to worry about."

Declan furrowed his eyebrows.

What is it now?" Lex asked, feigning annoyance.

"I just do not understand why she would risk her life to save me after all that has happened."

Lex began to shrug but stopped in the middle. "Oh geez! I can't believe I forgot." He turned and reached into his overnight bag and pulled out a little stuffed bear and a card. "She stopped by this morning and left you this. Maybe it will explain something." He handed them to Declan and plopped back down into his chair, pretending not to watch.

Declan picked up the little bear to get a better look at it. It was just a basic brown one, but it was wearing a little T-shirt that said, "I hope you get better beary soon!" He smiled and chuckled. Then he picked up the card and without warning his stomach began to churn as he realized that without the threat of the gang, Destiny had no reason to let him near her ever again. This card could be her final goodbye. He gulped and closed his eyes for a couple of seconds before gaining the determination to open up the envelope.

The front of the card was plain white with a simple picture of balloons, and the inside message was in Destiny's handwriting. Declan held his breath as he began to read.

> Declan,
> We have known each other for a long time, and I have thought of you as one of my closest friends. But, you betrayed me and hurt me.

Declan exhaled deliberately as tears brimmed in his eyes, but he forced himself to continue reading.

> I cannot yet forgive you for that, but for both of our sakes I pray that someday I can. However, this is not the reason I am writing to you. I am writing to you on behalf of

a Being to whom I owe everything, my Savior, Jesus Christ.

In our last conversation, you mentioned something about scales and earning your way into Heaven. This made it clear to me that you do not know Jesus as your Savior. It is because of my love for Christ that I could not let you die while I had the ability to give you more time to learn about Him. You see, there are no scales after death, and even the "tiniest" of sins needs to be paid for. No good deeds can undo the wrongs that have already been done, and if we have to pay for our sin ourselves, we will spend an eternity in Hell.

The good news is Jesus already paid for all our sins when He died on the cross. He purchased you and me with His blood so that we can go to Heaven and be with Him after we die. He wants to forgive you for every wrong you ever committed. You simply have to accept His payment as your own.

God loves you and wants you to be with Him, and if that gang had killed you before you got the chance to accept His forgiveness, not only would you suffer but God would have been robbed of something He desires, which is a relationship with you. So, even though my heart is still cold to you, I want you to understand that God's heart is always open.

This is why, as soon as the hospital lets me know you are healthy enough, I am going to come visit you with the intention of showing you, with my Bible, how you can know *you will go to Heaven when you die. If you do not wish for me to do this, then have Lex text me to let me know. Anyway, if I don't get a text saying otherwise, I will see you soon.*

Driven by the love of my Savior,
Destiny

Once Declan finished reading he pulled the letter to his chest and clutched it tight as tears rolled down his face. Then he closed his eyes and thought with a smile—*I am going to see her again. I get another chance. This time I will not make the same mistakes. This time, I will listen.*

Epilogue

WHAT WILL DESTINY show Declan?
Pull out a Bible and see for yourself.

1. There is no way a human being can be "good enough" to deserve to go to Heaven.

* Ecclesiastes 7:20: "There is not a righteous man on earth who does what is right and never sins."

* Isaiah 64:6: "All of us have become like one who is unclean, and all our righteous acts are like filthy rags; we all shrivel up like a leaf, and like the wind our sins sweep us away."

* Romans 3:10-18: "As it is written; 'There is no one righteous, not even one; there is no one who understands, no one who seeks God. All have turned away, they have together become worthless; there is no one who does good, not

even one. Their throats are open graves; their tongues practice deceit. The poison of vipers is on their lips. Their mouths are full of cursing and bitterness. Their feet are swift to shed blood; ruin and misery mark their ways, and the way of peace they do not know. There is no fear of God before their eyes.'"

2. So, what should we do? Try anyway? Follow the Law and Ten Commandments, which were given to Moses?

⚜ Romans 3:19-20: "Now we know that whatever the law says, it says to those who are under the law, so that every mouth may be silenced and the whole world held accountable to God. Therefore no one will be declared righteous in His sight by observing the law; rather, through the law we become conscious of sin."

⚜ Galatians 3:10-11: "All who rely on observing the law are under a curse, for it is written: 'Cursed is everyone who does not continue to do everything written in the Book of the Law.' Clearly no one is justified before God by the Law."

3. The only thing the Law does is give us a guideline which makes it clear we have messed up. Every time we break the Law we sin and God must punish sin because He is a just God.

⚜ Deuteronomy 32:4: "He is the Rock, His works are perfect, and all His ways are just. A faithful God who does no wrong, upright and just is He."

⚜ Romans 6:23: "For the wages of sin is death..."

4. Is there no hope? Since everyone has sinned and sin must be punished; how then can we be rescued?

- Romans 6:23: "For the wages of sin is death, but the gift of God is eternal life in Christ Jesus our Lord."
- Galatians 2:16: "Know that a man is not justified by observing the law, but by faith in Jesus Christ. So, we, too have put our faith in Christ Jesus that we may be justified by faith in Christ and not by observing the law, because by observing the law no one can be justified."

5. Just as Destiny said, God desires a relationship with you, and, because of this, He has fixed the sin problem and has paid the price for justice with His own blood.

- 2 Peter 4:9-10: "This is how God showed His love among us: He sent His one and only Son into the world that we might live through Him. This is love: not that we loved God, but that He loved us and sent His Son as an atoning sacrifice for our sins."
- John 3:16-18: "For God so loved the world that He gave His one and only Son, that whoever believes in Him shall not perish but have eternal life. For God did not send His Son into the world to condemn the world, but to save the world though Him. Whoever believes in Him is not condemned, but whoever does not believe stands condemned already because He has not believed in the name of God's one and only Son."

✿ Romans 5:6-8: "You see, at just the right time, when we were still powerless, Christ died for the ungodly. Very rarely will anyone die for a righteous man, though for a good man someone might possibly dare to die. But God demonstrates His own love for us in this: While we were still sinners, Christ died for us."

6. To become righteous (without any sin to pay for) in God's eyes we must believe that when Jesus died on the cross He paid the price for sin. This is a gift from God, and a true gift requires nothing in return. God did all of the work for us. We simply have to choose between accepting His payment for our sins or to keep on trying to pay for our sins ourselves.

✿ Romans 3:21-28: "But now a righteousness from God comes through faith in Jesus Christ to all who believe. There is no difference, for all have sinned and fall short of the glory of God, and are justified freely by His grace through the redemption that came by Christ Jesus. God presented Him as a sacrifice of atonement, through faith in His blood. He did this to demonstrate His justice, because in His forbearance He had left the sins committed beforehand, unpunished. He did this to demonstrate His justice at the present time, so as to be just and the One who justifies those who have faith in Jesus. Where then is boasting? It is excluded. On what principle? On that of observing the law? No, but on that of faith. For we maintain that a man is justified by faith apart from observing the law."

✳ Romans 4:4-5: "Now when a man works, His wages are not credited to him as a gift, but as an obligation. However, to the man who does not work but trusts God who justifies the wicked, His faith is credited as righteousness."

✳ John 14:6: "Jesus answered, 'I am the way the truth and the life. No one comes to the Father except through Me.'"

7. If we choose to accept Christ's payment for our sins, instead of trying to earn our way to Heaven by ourselves, we can be certain we will go to Heaven when we die.

✳ Romans 5:1-2: "Therefore, since we have been justified through faith, we have peace with God through our Lord Jesus Christ, through whom we have gained access by faith into this grace in which we now stand. And we rejoice in the hope of the glory of God."

✳ Titus 3:4-7: "But when the kindness and love of God our Savior appeared, He saved us, not because of righteous things we had done, but because of His mercy. He saved us through the washing of rebirth and the renewal by the Holy Spirit, whom He poured out on us generously through Jesus Christ our Savior, so that, having been justified by His grace, we might become heirs having the hope of eternal life."

✳ Hebrews 7:23-28: "… Now there have been many of those priests (High Priests of the Old Testament), since death prevented them from continuing in office; but because Jesus lives forever, He has a permanent priesthood. Therefore, He is able to save completely those who come to God through Him, because He always lives to intercede for them. Such a High Priest meets our need—one who is holy, blameless, pure, set apart from sinners, exalted above the heavens. Unlike the other High Priests, He does not need to offer sacrifices day after day, first for His own sins, and then for the sins of the people. He sacrificed for their sins once for all when He offered Himself. For the Law appoints as High Priests men who are weak; but the oath, which came after the Law, appointed the Son, who has been made perfect forever."

God gave us all free will so that we may choose to accept His free gift of an eternal relationship with Him. But we may also choose not to accept it and to pay the price for sin on our own; because love means nothing if there is not an alternate option. I, for one, will be praying that you choose to accept God's gift; then perhaps someday you and I may meet in the life to come.

With my utmost sincerity,
Amanda Hovseth

ACKNOWLEDGEMENTS

I THANK MY parents, Dan and Lori Hovseth, for supporting me in my writing and my decision to work at getting published. I thank my pastor, Rich Peterson, for leading my dad to a saving knowledge of Jesus Christ and as a result turning around the life of every person in my family. I thank these same three for reading my manuscript and verifying the accuracy of its theology.

Thanks to Starr Wiebe for being with me literally every step of the way with every decision I made during the creating of this story. Thanks to Kristine Lewis for listening to me ramble on about my story ideas and reading my manuscript. Thanks to many other friends who have been there for me through life so far, but special thanks to Emily Holscher, Emily Burkey, Sarah Ross, and Lisa Osler for taking time out of their own lives to give me input on this book and listening to me as I sorted through my thoughts.

Shout out to my siblings: Kara, Giles, and Gavin Hovseth. Love you guys!

ABOUT THE AUTHOR

AMANDA STUDIED Biblical Studies at New Tribes Bible Institute in Waukesha, WI were she expanded her knowledge of how God has chosen to work in the world and of how unbelievably expansive His love is. She then studied creative writing at the University of Nebraska in Lincoln where she worked in the Writing Center, edited for the Daily Nebraskan, and took all the writing and reading classes they had to offer before moving on when they tried to peer pressure her into paying for the pleasure of taking excessive math and science classes.

She now owns and operates Synecdoche Publishing, LLC and continues to write, because if she were to stop, her brain might explode. She has been published by various publishers, including the University of Nebraska Press in their book *Voices of Nebraska: Diverse Landscapes, Diverse Peoples*, but has started to mostly focus on writing and editing for her own company.

This book, *Perspective: A Dark Tale of Hope*, has been previously published by two other publishers but Amanda eventually re-gained the rights to it so that she could publish this edition through her own company.

She wishes everyone who reads her books, good fortune, and everyone who doesn't, slightly-less-but-still-good fortune.

Follow her on Instagram: @mandy_jh7
Visit her Facebook page: @amandahovseth